LACE

THE JUST THIS ONCE SERIES

DEBORAH BLADON

CHAPTER ONE

Olivia

"I NEED you to tell me who these panties belong to."

I turn at the sound of the masculine voice. It's not that it's a rarity here. It's a lingerie boutique, so we have our share of male clientele, but this voice is different.

It's edged with a roughness that speaks of confidence and control.

"You want me to what?" Liza, the newly hired sales associate, asks.

"You heard me." The man barks back, an added note of irritation in his tone. "I need to know who bought this pair of panties because she's a goddamn thief."

I move across the boutique, my nude heels clicking a quick beat on the hardwood floors.

I stop when I catch sight of the back of the man attached to the voice.

He's tall. I'd guess around six-foot-two. His shoulders are broad, his brown hair long enough to skim the collar of the white dress shirt he's wearing. The sleeves are rolled up to reveal muscular forearms that pop in and out of view when he moves his arms.

I should visit this store more often. Working from the corporate offices of Liore Lingerie isn't nearly as exciting as this.

"Can I help you, sir?" I call out from behind him, running a hand over my long dark hair. "I'm Olivia Hull. I'm the District Operations Manager of Liore Lingerie."

He turns.

Holy hell.

It's as if a sculptor created the perfect man and dropped him in front of me.

Impeccable bone structure, a strong jaw, a sharp nose and the pièce de résistance; two of the bluest eyes I've ever seen.

"Are you in charge?" He looks me over.

I do the same to him, stopping to linger at the barest hint of smooth skin beneath the unbuttoned collar of his shirt. "If there's a problem, I can help."

A ball of black lace falls from his hand onto the checkout counter. "Give me the name of the woman who bought these."

I move around the counter until I'm facing him directly. I glance down at the lace. "We sell hundreds of pairs of panties every day, sir."

He shoves the lace closer to me. "I don't care how many you sell. I only care about who you sold this pair to."

I grab a silver pen from the top of the counter and tug on the edge of the lace. "This is one of our most popular styles of panties. We have several stores here in Manhattan. It's impossible to pinpoint who these belong to."

"You must have records." He points at the computer sitting atop the counter. "She told me they were brand new.

Key in the code or whatever it is you do when you sell a pair and print me out the names of the women who have bought them in the last few days. She's about your height, blonde, with brown eyes."

Liza moves toward the computer, but I stop her with a hand on her wrist. "We value the privacy of each of our customers. We would never compromise that for any reason, sir."

"Your customer," he drags the last word across his tongue with disdain. "Your customer took a very valuable item from my apartment last night after I fell asleep. She was in such a rush to steal my property that she forgot those in my bed."

"Why don't you just ask her to give it back?" Liza laughs. "Call her up and tell her that you'll exchange the panties for whatever it is she took."

Oh, poor naïve Liza.

"I take it that you don't know her name?" I cross my arms over my chest. The motion stretches the fabric of my black sheath dress taut across my breasts.

His eyes drop to my arms. "That's correct."

"I'm afraid we can't help you." I slide the panties back across the counter with a push of the pen. "I'd suggest that you return to wherever it was that you met her. With any luck, you'll cross paths with her again."

"That's your advice?" He points at the windows that over-look Fifth Avenue. "Millions of women live in this city. How am I going to find her?"

I narrow my blue eyes and study him. "I don't have a clue."

"You need to do better than that." His expression turns smug, which only makes him that much sexier. "You need to get on that computer and find out who she is."

"It's not my job to track down your one-night stand, sir."

He rests both of his palms on the counter and leans closer to me. "I'm going to take this above your head."

"You're more than welcome to do that." I smile sweetly. "I should warn you that our entire management team are committed to our customers and the security of their personal information."

"Your customer stole an autographed Trey Hale jersey from me last night." He scoops the panties back into his hand and shoves them into the front pocket of his black pants. "In case you don't know who that is, Trey Hale is a professional baseball player. He's the best pitcher in the league. He won the World Series last year."

I know exactly who Trey Hale is, but I won't tell this arrogant jerk that.

"Your superiors will be hearing about this, Ms. Hull," he calls over his shoulder as he starts toward the exit. "That jersey was meant to be a gift for my nephew's tenth birthday and your refusal to cooperate with me is the reason he'll be disappointed."

I sigh. Why the hell did the beautiful bastard have to tell me that?

"How is it our fault that his random one-night stand lifted that jersey?" Liza asks as she sprays disinfectant on the top of the counter. "He shouldn't take strangers home with him."

I don't weigh in on that since I've been guilty of inviting a one-night stand back to my place. Luckily for me, that guy didn't help himself to anything but a bowl of cereal the next morning.

"Did he mention his name to you at all?" I question her as I watch her swirl the disinfectant in a circle with a paper towel, her red hair bouncing around her shoulders. "Did he tell it to you before I came over?"

She looks at me. "No. I would have remembered if he did."

I could forget he ever walked in here, and I would if it weren't for the mention of his nephew. I can replace that jersey within the hour. All I need to do is give my cousin, Trey, a call and I'll have an autographed jersey, baseball and two tickets to a game in my hand in the time it takes me to get to his apartment.

"I should have asked for his name," I say, picking up a stack of gift cards to place on a display near the entrance.

"That slice of heaven was Alexander Donato." A woman approaches the checkout counter with several pieces of lingerie in her hands. "I know exactly where you can find him, or at least a picture of him. His handsome face is on a billboard in the middle of Times Square."

CHAPTER TWO

OLIVIA

"I CAN RUN down to Times Square and find the billboard," Liza says, as soon as the customer is headed toward the boutique's doors with her purchases neatly folded in tissue paper inside two peach colored Liore bags. "He must be famous. Why else would he be on a billboard?"

I'm surprised she kept it together as long as she did. After the customer mentioned Alexander Donato's name and the billboard in Times Square, Liza wanted more details.

I changed the subject.

The woman had traveled to New York City from Texas for her birthday. The lingerie was a gift she was giving to herself. I wanted her visit to the boutique to be extra special, so I offered a birthday discount on her entire purchase.

I used my employee code and took over the checkout process myself.

My goal was for the woman to walk out with a memory of a shopping experience that far surpassed her expectations.

When our boutique in Dallas opens next year, my hope is that she'll become a regular customer who sings our praises to anyone who will listen.

I tug my phone out of the pocket of my dress. "Steph mentioned that a shipment of silk pajamas just arrived. They need to be unpacked and steamed. You can handle that, right?"

When I worked at this boutique as a sales associate, Steph did the same. She's worked her way up to the manager's position and she loves it. She's doing a great job, considering Liza is a handful of misplaced energy.

"I want to know more about Alexander." She bats her long eyelashes and flips her hair over her shoulder. "He's insanely hot and I could feel something happening between us."

I skim my fingers over my phone's screen. I'm silent while I scan the results of a quick search of the jerk that Liza is swooning over.

I can't blame her. There was something alluring about him.

Apparently, a lot of women feel the same way I do based on the size of his official online fan club.

I click on his personal website.

"He was born here in New York City thirty-five-years ago," I say as I read the bio page.

"Yum." Liza bumps her shoulder against mine. "That makes him twelve years older than me."

And eight years older than me.

"I have a thing for older guys." She giggles. "They're wise and they make the best lovers."

I wouldn't know. I once dated a guy who was three years older than me and the sex wasn't spectacular. That's the biggest age gap I've ever experienced. "Wisdom doesn't always come with age, Liza."

She nods. "You're right. The last guy I slept with was thirty-six. He wasn't a genius, but he did know what he was doing in bed."

I look down at my phone. "He's a conductor. It says that he's won prestigious awards and has studied with some of the best classical musicians in the world. He's guest conducting the Philharmonic starting next month."

"Alexander is a conductor?" She fans herself. "I could tell he was sophisticated. He had that air about him. You know what I mean, Olivia. Don't you?"

All I know is that he was stuck-up and smug. He's good-looking, but that doesn't make up for being demanding and unreasonable.

Still, a part of me feels a pull to do the right thing and call my cousin, Trey.

Alexander's nephew shouldn't miss out on his birthday gift because his uncle took a thief to bed.

"I know that your boss is looking over here and wondering what you're doing." I wave a hand in the air at Steph.

Liza glances over her shoulder and tosses Steph a wave herself. "As soon as my shift is over, I'm going to Times Square to see that billboard and then I'm going to buy a ticket to the Philharmonic."

I'm going home and since my apartment isn't anywhere near Times Square, I won't be subjected to a larger than life size image of Alexander Donato.

I've seen enough of that man for one day.

———

"SO, HYPOTHETICALLY SPEAKING..."

"Olivia, every time you start a sentence with that, you're about to ask a question about yourself. " Kate Wesley, my friend and neighbor, interrupts me. Smiling, she tosses a piece of popcorn into her mouth. "Cut the bullshit, and get to the point."

I pull my legs up and curl them under me.

We're sitting on my couch watching our favorite show on Netflix. It may be Friday night, but neither of us had plans, so when Kate caught sight of me sliding my key into the lock on my apartment door, she opened her door and asked if I was up for movie night.

We live directly across the hall from one another and ever since I moved in eight months ago, Kate has become a good friend to me.

What started as a bad habit of us spying on each other through the peepholes in our doors has turned into a sister-like bond.

"I already know what you're going to tell me to do, Kate."

"The right thing?" She arches a brow. "I always tell you to do the right thing."

She does. Kate is my go-to if I ever need advice about anything.

I tug on the end of her blonde braid. That draws her gaze back to me from the television set. "What is it, Liv?"

I see the concern in her hazel eyes. Kate isn't just one of the most beautiful people I've ever met. She's also the kindest.

"It's not anything serious," I reassure her with a weak smile. "I was doing some work at one of the boutiques today and a man came in with a pair of panties that a woman had left at his place."

She crosses her legs, angling them toward me. She's

dressed in a pair of black yoga pants and an oversized red sweatshirt that's the same hue as the T-shirt I have on. We both opted for comfortable tonight.

"I'm dying to find out what part of this you need advice on." She laughs. "Unless you know the guy with the panties. He wasn't an ex of yours, was he?"

I shake my head. "Hell, no."

"So what happened?" She blinks." What did he want?"

"The names of all the women who have bought a pair of black panties from Liore in the last few days."

Her hand darts into the air. "I bought a pair from the Charming Collection at the boutique in Tribeca last Monday."

Smiling, I narrow my eyes at her. "You didn't hook up with a man last night and steal his autographed Trey Hale baseball jersey, did you?"

"I wish." She shoots me a look. "I wish I had hooked up with a man and I don't need to steal a Hale jersey. If I want one, all I have to do is ask you to get one from your cousin for me."

I glance at the television. "The autographed jersey was for the guy's nephew. It was going to be a gift for his tenth birthday, but his one-night stand took off with it and left behind her panties."

"I get it," she says with a jerk of her chin. "You're wondering if you should call Trey and ask for a new jersey for the nephew's birthday. Is that it?"

"I don't know this man." I sigh and lean my head back on my plush vintage blue velvet couch. "He was so arrogant and rude. He threatened to go over my head at work because I wouldn't help him track down his one-night stand. Part of me is wondering why I'm even considering doing him a favor."

She taps my knee to get me to look at her. I do.

"The other part of you is thinking about how that boy will

feel when he opens his birthday gift and finds an autographed Hale jersey." She turns back to face the television. "You're not doing Mr. Arrogant a favor. You're making a ten-year-old crazy happy on his birthday."

She's right. I'll find a way to get a new jersey to Alexander Donato. He never has to know that it came from me.

CHAPTER THREE

ALEXANDER

"WHEN'S MONTE due back in New York?"

My sister, Phoebe Costa, rolls her eyes. "Why do you insist on asking that question every time I invite you over for dinner?"

I push the empty plate in front of me to the side. "Why do you insist on avoiding the question?"

She's twenty-eight-years-old, a mom, and a third-grade teacher, but my sister still knows exactly how to annoy the hell out of me. Her tried-and-true approach of answering a question with a question irritates me, which is why she's become an expert at it.

"I don't want Alvin to overhear this conversation." She glances over her shoulder at her son's closed bedroom door. "Imagine you're an almost ten-year-old kid and your father can only carve out two days a month for you."

I can't imagine it. I don't want Alvin to live it, but his dad is a truck driver. He's on the road constantly to help put food on the kitchen table in this two-bedroom house in Queens.

Phoebe was pregnant before she graduated from high school. Monte never wavered in his commitment to her and their baby.

They got married at city hall, Phoebe pushed back her college start date by a semester and with the help of Monte's family, they flourished.

I wasn't around.

I was in Europe studying piano and cello. That morphed into a passion for conducting which took me on a whirlwind tour of the globe.

I offered my support in the form of birthday and Christmas gifts sent from wherever I was.

Getting to know my nephew is my priority now that I'm renting an apartment in Manhattan.

"Monte isn't sure he'll make it back in time for Alvin's birthday next week." She twirls a strand of her blonde hair around her finger. "I convinced Alvin to invite a few of his friends from school over for pizza and birthday cake, but he's going to be heartbroken if his dad doesn't show."

I don't blame the kid.

"It's a week from tomorrow. You'll be here, right?" Her blue eyes latch onto mine. "You're Alvin's hero, Alex. He's named after you."

I laugh. "Monte told me you named him after me and his oldest brother, Vincent."

"Since when do you listen to my husband," she scoffs. "Alvin looks up to you. You're the reason he loves playing piano."

"He hates playing piano."

"He hates it this week," she clarifies with a smile. "How

can piano compete with baseball when his favorite team is headed to the World Series?"

I scrub my hands over my face. I don't need the reminder that my nephew loves the game and the pitcher who won the series last year.

An autographed Trey Hale jersey was up for auction last week at a charity event I attended. I outbid every other person in the room. Even if the money hadn't been going to a worthwhile cause, I would have paid whatever it took to get my hands on it.

Alvin worships Hale and the jersey was supposed to be the first gift I've ever given my nephew face-to-face.

That plan was screwed up by my need to fuck a random woman last night.

Phoebe and I both turn at the sound of Alvin's bedroom door opening. "Mom, I'm done my homework. I'll load the dishwasher and then can I play a video game?"

"I still can't believe you sent him to do his homework after dinner. He had all weekend to get it done." I stand and grab my empty plate. "You're a hard-ass."

Alvin picks up Phoebe's plate and his. He looks up at me. "You have no idea, Alex."

Alex. I've always been Alex to this kid. The uncle designation is reserved for Monte's brothers. They've been in his life from day one.

"You'll fill me in sometime." I nod toward the kitchen. "Let's get the dishes done so you'll have more time before bed to battle whatever demon is in your game."

"It's not a demon." He moves to walk in front of me. "I'm more into strategy games. I like things that challenge me."

So do I.

That's why I've been thinking about the woman from the lingerie store.

Olivia Hull is beautiful and gutsy. The no-nonsense approach she took with me was as much of a turn-on as an annoyance.

I'll take her advice and head back to the club where I met the woman I fucked last night. I hope to hell I'll have the Hale jersey back in my hand before this day is over.

———

"THIS WAS YOUR IDEA, ALEXANDER." Jack Pearce looks down at the watch on his wrist. "You're late."

Tossing my friend a smile, I pat him on the back. "I was in Queens having dinner with my sister and her son."

He hands me a bottle of imported beer as I take a seat next to him. "I took the liberty of ordering for you."

I'm grateful.

After I hopped on the subway and made it back to Manhattan, I hit up my place for a shower and change of clothes.

I traded the black dress pants and white button-down shirt for a pair of dark jeans and a black sweater.

Jack's dressed in a two-piece gray suit and white dress shirt. It's his standard attire on any given weekday.

He's sporting a light growth of beard and his black hair is in need of a cut. His green eyes are zeroed in on my face.

He looks like he could use a visit to a barber and some sleep.

The man manages other people's fortunes and as long as I've known him, his job is his life.

He's on call twenty-four seven for all of his clients. I count myself among them.

We started as friends back in college and when I tasted

success, it was Jack I turned to for guidance. He keeps my finances healthy so I can focus on building my career.

"I read your text." He shakes his head as he surveys the packed dance floor. "Let me get the facts straight."

I take a pull of the beer, knowing that he's going to offer advice I haven't asked for.

"You met a woman at this club last night. You took her home and fucked her. When you dozed off she left without her panties, but not before she helped herself to a baseball jersey you left in plain sight."

I tip my bottle of beer in the air. "That sums it up."

His gaze darts from the dance floor back to me. We're in a private VIP area that Jack has access to. Last night I was on my own. I knew what I wanted so my time spent in the club was limited to just shy of thirty minutes.

That's all it took for me to find a willing, unattached blonde.

"I take it the police aren't working hard on the case?"

"I see no reason to involve them." I wave away the idea with a brush of my hand in the air.

He lets out a laugh. "It's their job."

"I'm not saying that something like this would draw the interest of the press, Jack." I take a drink. "It's a stolen baseball jersey, not a Rolex, but I don't want any unnecessary publicity before..."

"Before you take the stage next month?" He arches a dark brow. "I get it. You're trying to keep a low profile."

I pause. "Chances are the jersey will show up on an online auction site or at a pawn shop. I don't have time to hunt it down. I'm here tonight to see if the woman I took home last night shows. If she does, I'll convince her to give it back if she still has it."

"Or she'll convince you to buy it back for the right price."

He looks over at the dance floor again. "Give me a description of her."

"She's in her early thirties, maybe five-foot-four or five, blonde hair halfway down her back, brown eyes." I close my eyes in an attempt to stir my memory. "She has a tattoo on her left wrist. I think it's an arrow."

"I can work with that." He pushes up from the bar stool and buttons his suit jacket. "Let's divide and conquer. If your little thief is here, we'll find her."

CHAPTER FOUR

OLIVIA

I STEP into my cousin Trey's loft and freeze.

I saw this place when he first bought it a year ago. Back then it was one big space with exposed brick walls and overhead wooden beams.

When he came over to my apartment one Saturday afternoon during the off-season, I forced him to watch a marathon of home improvement and design shows with me in the hope that he'd get inspired and transform his empty loft into a home.

He did.

The loft now has defined areas, including a massive chef's kitchen, a living room with a gas fireplace and what I presume to be a large master suite down a wide hallway.

It's decorated tastefully in earthy masculine tones, unlike the eclectic mix of antique and thrift store finds that I've furnished my apartment with.

"You're here." Trey shuts the door behind me. "How's my favorite cousin?"

I sigh when he pulls me into a tight embrace.

He's always been more like a brother to me than a cousin. Our mothers are sisters and we grew up spending every vacation together.

I pull back and look up into his dark eyes. "I'm good. What about you? You're the one who is balancing the hopes of an entire city on your shoulders."

"I play the best game I can every time. With any luck, we win some." He laughs as he motions toward the kitchen. "I'll grab you a can of that soda you like."

I'm touched that he remembers. "I didn't take you away from anything important, did I?"

He glances back at me as he pours the soda into a tall glass. "I had practice this morning. I'm going over a few things with my agent this afternoon, but he's in the office on a call."

He points toward the hallway.

I glance in that direction as I curl my hand around the glass. "I hope you know that I wouldn't have asked for you to sign a jersey for just anyone, but as I said on the phone last night, it's for a ten-year-old boy."

I called Trey before Kate left my apartment.

I explained that I briefly met someone who had one of his autographed jerseys, but it had been stolen. Before I could get another word out, Trey told me to stop by this afternoon to pick up a replacement.

"I'm happy to help out, Olivia." He reaches into the back pocket of his jeans to tug out his cell phone. "My mom sent me a picture this morning."

I smile when he turns the phone around. It's a picture of our moms on a beach in Hawaii. They bought a timeshare on

Maui a few years ago and they take advantage of it as often as they can in the fall and winter.

The rest of their time is spent in a condo in Boston.

Both of our moms are widowed and their shared grief forged a close bond between the two of them.

I don't remember my dad since he died before my fifth birthday, but Trey's dad was a driving force in my life until he passed ten years ago.

"Look how tanned they are." I laugh. "They're living their best lives right now."

"As they should." He leans his forearms on the kitchen island. "Are you living your best life?"

I pull on the arm of my off-the-shoulder gray sweater. I slid it on after my yoga class ended thirty minutes ago.

I thought about going home to shower and change into something more presentable than the fraying sweater and gray yoga pants I'm wearing, but Trey has seen me at my absolute worst. I knew he wouldn't care what I look like.

"Hale." A man's voice calls from behind me. "You didn't tell me that we were expecting company."

I turn to the sight of a gray-haired man dressed in navy blue slacks and a light blue V-neck sweater. Silver rimmed eyeglasses sit on his nose.

"This is my cousin." Trey drops a hand on my shoulder. "Olivia, this is my agent."

"Buck Remsen." The man pushes a hand at me. "I finally get to meet the Olivia Hull."

I take his hand for a quick shake before I gaze back at Trey. "The Olivia Hull?"

My cousin rakes a hand through his hair. It's the same shade as mine. "I talk about you from time-to-time. All good things, Livi."

I smile at the nickname his dad gave me with when we were kids.

"From what I've heard, you're the one who coached him to be the player that he is today," Buck says with a gleam in his eye.

I toss my head back in laughter.

"Don't laugh, Olivia." Trey chuckles. "You were the only person who would stand at home plate so I could practice pitching."

"You were seven and I was five." I hold up my hand, wiggling my fingers. "To be clear, Trey, I'd never do it now."

"Neither would I." Buck opens the fridge and takes out a bottle of water. "I want to see my next birthday, so I'm never getting in front of one of your curve balls."

"Olivia is here to pick up the jersey I signed earlier." Trey rounds the island I'm standing next to.

"For the kid?" Buck takes a swallow of water. "I was on the phone just now arranging club seats for game one of the series for him and a guest. We'll have a gift pack waiting there for him."

"A gift pack?" I ask, looking at Buck.

"The autographed jersey and a ball signed by the team." Buck smiles, tugging a phone from the pocket of his jacket. "We'll throw in a cap and a varsity jacket. This kid is going to have a birthday he'll never forget."

This goes above and beyond what I requested. "I don't know what to say."

"What's the boy's name?" Buck's gaze drops to his phone. "We'll give him a Hale jersey, but we'll personalize the jacket for him."

"I don't know his name," I confess softly. "I know his uncle's name. He's the one who had his autographed jersey stolen."

"What's the uncle's name?" Trey asks.

"Alexander Donato," I answer quickly.

Buck's head pops up, his brown eyes searching my face. "The conductor? It's his nephew?"

I nod.

"Who?" Trey's brow furrows. "I've never heard the name before."

"Learn it quick." Buck's mouth slides into a wide smile. "You're going to do a meet and greet with Donato and his nephew before the big game and with any luck, a video capture of that will go viral."

Shit. My well-intentioned gesture is turning into a publicity stunt.

"When you talk to Alexander about this, can you give him my number?" Buck holds up his phone. "Trey will text it to you."

Trey's fingers tap out something on his phone before mine buzzes.

I look down at it and the New York based number my cousin just texted me.

Sucking in a deep breath, I lower myself onto one of the stools next to the island. "I'd prefer if Alexander didn't know I was involved in any of this. Is there a way we can do that?"

"She's humble." Trey looks back and forth between Buck and me. "Olivia has never been one to shine a spotlight on herself."

It's a welcome compliment, but it has nothing to do with my desire to stay out of this. I don't want Alexander Donato to know that I went to any trouble for him. He strikes me as the type of man who would misinterpret a helping hand for something more.

I don't need him to jump to any conclusions about my good intentions or me.

All I wanted was an autographed jersey to replace the one his one-night stand ran off with.

I was going to shove it in a plain envelope, address it to him in care of the Philharmonic, and mail it to their administrative office.

That was before it turned into a baseball lover's dream gift.

Buck stares at me. "I'll have my assistant take care of all of it. She'll never bring your name into it."

"Thank you." I breathe a sigh of relief. "Thank you both for everything."

CHAPTER FIVE

ALEXANDER

"IS THIS A JOKE?" I stare at the tall blonde woman standing in front of me. "Who the hell sent you here?"

"I'm not joking," she says, her voice trembling. "I told you that my boss, Buck Remsen, asked me to contact you. He represents Trey Hale."

I didn't believe it the first time she said it, and I sure as hell don't believe it now.

This woman tapped on my shoulder as I was waiting for my double shot of espresso at a café around the corner from my apartment.

I skimmed her face and the light blue sweater dress she's wearing trying to jog my memory into giving me a name. Her name.

I assumed I'd met her at some point in the past, but as soon as she started talking, I realized that I'd never seen her before.

She introduced herself as Melody something-or-other. I

didn't catch her surname because the barista barked out "*Alex*" and I reached for my order.

Melody went on to explain that she had a surprise for me.

I waited with baited breath and raised brows for her to continue.

She tripped over her own words as she spit out that her boss arranged for a day at the ballpark for my nephew. I didn't hear anything after she said that she heard that my Trey Hale jersey was stolen and that a guy named Buck wants to replace it. She mentioned tickets to a game and a personalized baseball jacket. If this is legitimate, it's going to paste a permanent smile on Alvin's face and cement my position as the *best uncle who ever lived.*

"I left two messages with your manager yesterday." Melody sighs. "You're a tough man to get in touch with, Mr. Donato."

That's by design.

I'm glad to hear that Vito, my manager, is doing his job and acting as a buffer between anyone I don't personally know and me.

I sip the coffee, debating whether or not Melody is indeed here to offer me the experience of a lifetime for Alvin, or if she's a friend of the thief who stole my jersey. Given the proximity of this café to my apartment, I can't be sure.

I've been irritated since Jack and I came up empty at the club on Friday night. I've spent the three days since immersed in work, while Jack hit up every store in the five boroughs that sells sports memorabilia. I didn't ask him to search for the stolen jersey, but he knows how much my nephew means to me. Unfortunately, he struck out.

The blonde clears her throat, so I face her. "How did you find me?"

Her gaze darts to the line of people waiting to place their

orders. "I joined your online fan club yesterday morning. I read through every post."

I know a fan club exists. I've never taken a look at it. I focus on the job, and the benefits that come with it, which often includes the company of a beautiful woman for a night.

Beyond that, I don't give a fuck what people are saying about me. I grew a thick skin after my first solo cello performance in Berlin years ago. The reviews tore me to shreds. I trashed my dressing room, downed a bottle of whiskey and vowed never to let another person's opinion impact my craft again.

"Someone posted that they saw you in here yesterday morning around this time." She shrugs. "I thought it was worth a try."

It's a plausible explanation, but I'm still skeptical.

I call her bluff because I need to move my day forward and I can't do that standing in this café. "I want to talk to your boss. Buck? Is that his name?"

"Buck Remsen." She smiles. "If you give me your number I'll have him call you…"

"No." I narrow my eyes. "Give me his number."

She spits out a ten-digit number before my phone is out of my pocket.

"Repeat that."

She doesn't hesitate. She relays each number to me again, slowly and clearly.

"I'll give him a call," I say after I program the number into my phone under the contact name *Buck*.

"He's in the office all day today if you'd rather speak to him in person." She eyes my coffee cup. "I'm heading back there after I grab a latte. We can share a ride."

"Where's the office?" I ask because there's zero chance in

hell that I'm getting in a cab with her. I'm still unsure if this Buck character is real.

"Lexington and Forty-Sixth Street." Her gaze scans the large menu board behind me. "It's the Remsen Agency building. You can't miss it."

I head straight for the exit.

It's time for a quick online search of Buck Remsen. If he checks out, I'll be shaking the man's hand within the hour.

———

"MY EX-WIFE WOULD HAVE KILLED for a chance to meet you."

It's not the greeting I was expecting from Buck Remsen, but I'll take it. The gray-haired man is indeed Trey Hale's agent and if the evidence I found online of that wasn't enough, this office is.

There are framed photographs of Buck with some of the biggest names in sports today, and yesterday. The picture of him and Hale is front and center.

His reputation for being cutthroat in negotiations on behalf of his clients was evident in the two archived New York Times articles I read on my phone during the cab ride over here.

If he had any experience in the realm of the arts, I'd be tempted to fire my representation and convince him to take me on.

"You're not an easy guy to track down, Alex."

I don't mind the familiarity. Hell, I welcome it. This guy has a direct connection to Alvin's hero. It seems that Melody was speaking the truth back at the café.

"I'm a busy man." I laugh. "You can relate, Buck."

"One day." He holds a hand in the air. "One day I'll leave this earth. That'll be the day I relax."

This guy is hardcore to the extreme. I try to carve out time in my schedule for relaxation at least a few times a week. My frequent visits to Phoebe's place usually top the list when I have a spare hour or two.

I cut to the chase because I came here for one reason only and that's not idle chatter. "When I spoke to Melody she mentioned a surprise for my nephew."

"What's his name?" He lifts his chin in the air. "I need the kid's name."

I don't question what for because this guy represents one of the greatest pitchers to ever take to the mound. "Alvin Costa."

He reaches for a pen and a pad of paper sitting on his desk. He writes down something. I'm going to assume it's Alvin's name. I take that as a good sign.

"Look, Alex." He leans his hand against the desk. "I'm going to be straight with you."

I cross my arms over my chest and nod, unsure of what he's about to say. "Please. Go ahead."

"When Trey found out that the signed jersey you bought for Alvin was stolen, he wanted to step up and do the right thing." He glances at the framed photograph of him and Trey. "Trey loved the game when he was a kid too and he knows how much the jersey will mean to Alvin, but he wants to do more."

"More?" I question.

"We want to get Alvin down to the park for the first game of the World Series." He clears his throat. "I'm talking two club seats, refreshments, the jersey, a team jacket, some pennants. Hell, we'll give the kid a ball signed by the team."

I sense a *but* coming.

Buck delivers it with ease. "All we need from you is twenty minutes with Trey and a few dozen cameras. You bring Alvin to the locker room before the first pitch is thrown, we do a quick interview on camera for the local news, snap some pictures and you're free to enjoy the game with your nephew."

I get it. They want the opportunity to showcase Trey Hale's benevolence. "I'll have to run it by Alvin's mom, but I don't see a problem."

He claps his hands together. "Looks like Alvin's going to have a birthday to remember. I'll need your direct number so we can arrange all the details."

I text a simple, *thank you*, to the number Melody gave me at the café.

Buck's phone beeps. "Got it. I'll be in touch, Alex."

It's my cue to leave, but I'm not about to. I welcome the effort he's putting in to make Alvin's birthday one for the record books, but I want to know who the hell is behind this.

I wait a beat and then casually ask the question I've wanted to know the answer to since I walked into this office and saw the picture of Hale on the wall. "How did you hear about the stolen jersey, Buck?"

He glances at me. "Does it matter?"

It shouldn't, but it does. Jack would have told me if he had a connection this close to Trey Hale. He knew I was on the hunt for an autographed jersey for months.

The only other people who know that a one-night stand left my place with the jersey are the women who work at the lingerie boutique and the half dozen customers who were there the morning I stormed in with those panties in my hand demanding answers.

"It matters," I answer succinctly.

"I gave her my word that I wouldn't bring her name into

this." He pushes his glasses up the bridge of his nose. "She's close to Trey, so I don't want to rock the boat. He puts family first. He'll have my head if he knows I broke my promise to her."

Her.

"They're family?" I push for more.

He nods. "That's all you're getting out of me."

It's not enough, but I sense that his loyalty to Trey will outweigh the two tickets to a performance of the symphony I was about to tempt him with. I'll still have the tickets sent over to him with a note thanking him for what he's doing for Alvin.

"Fair enough." I pocket my phone.

I'll have to figure out the identity of the mystery woman on my own.

CHAPTER SIX

OLIVIA

I TAKE A TENTATIVE SIP. A smile of satisfaction blooms on my lips. "You're right, Steph. This smoothie is amazing."

"I know. That's mango pineapple. Mine is strawberry banana." She places her cup on the corner of my desk. "I thought my roommate was crazy when she told me that she quit her nine-to-five to start selling smoothies from a food cart in Washington Square Park. I'm beginning to think she's a genius."

"I'm not one for throwing caution to the wind, but I think she made the right choice." I eye the logo on the side of the plastic cup. "You're not here to tell me that you're jumping ship so you can sell smoothies too, are you?"

Her mouth twists into a wry grin. "If that was the case, would you give me a raise to keep me?"

I would. Since Steph took over as the manager of Liore's flagship store, employee turnover is down and sales are up. We need her and a raise in pay was already in her near future. I was going to break the good news to her a few weeks from now during her yearly employee evaluation.

"You're due for a five percent raise next month, but I'm willing to increase that to seven percent if you sign a new two-year contract with us today."

"Are you serious?" She inches forward on the white leather chair that's in front of my desk. "Really?"

"Tell me you'll stay, Steph."

"I'm staying. I'm not going anywhere," she says hurriedly. "I'll sign the contract today."

I drop my gaze before I lock eyes with her. "You didn't come here to quit, did you?"

She breathes a sigh. "I didn't. I hope that doesn't change your offer. I'm committed one hundred percent to Liore. I love my job."

"It doesn't change a thing. The raise is yours." I take another sip of the smoothie. "Did you stop by just to share the smoothie?"

"No." She tucks a strand of her blonde hair behind her ear. "Something happened at the boutique this morning. I thought you should know about it. I wanted to tell you in person."

Eighteen months ago, when I first took on this position, I would have felt a jolt of panic at those words, but a lot has changed since then. I've learned that every problem has a solution. "What happened, Steph?"

"Alexander Donato happened." She rolls her blue eyes. "He showed up again demanding more information."

"What information?" I ask as I feel a tense knot forming deep in my stomach.

I think I already know the answer to that question.

Trey sent me a text early this morning telling me that

Buck had met with Alexander yesterday to give him the good news about the jersey and the tickets to a game.

I replied that I was glad and I asked Trey if Buck kept my name out of it.

Trey assured me that he had.

I trust Trey, but I don't know Buck. Maybe he let something slip to Alexander about me.

"He asked if I was related to Trey Hale." She shoots me an amused look. "He asked Liza too. Thankfully, she has no idea that you're Trey's cousin."

I breathe a heavy sigh of relief. "Thank you for not saying anything."

"When you first told me that he was your cousin, I promised you that I'd keep that information to myself." She raises her hand in the air as if she's taking a vow. "I don't break promises, Olivia."

"So he left the store after that?"

Her hand curls around her smoothie cup. "He tried to, but Liza was determined to flirt with him."

I can't hide my smile. "She's crushing hard on him."

"He wasn't feeling it." She grins at me. "He asked about you before he left."

The knot in my stomach morphs into an annoying flutter in my chest. I try to chase it away with a cough, but it does little good.

"He wanted to know how he could reach you," she goes on, "I asked if there was a message that I could relay to you and he said he'd deliver it himself."

"Himself?" I blurt out. "Did you tell him where he could find me?"

She shakes her head. "No, but all he would need to do is look at the Liore corporate website. Your bio page has your office phone number on it and the address of this building."

She's right.

If Alexander is determined to talk to me, he'll have no trouble finding me.

———

"THIS IS the guy who waltzed into Liore last week with a pair of panties in his hand?" Kate hands my phone back to me. "He's super hot, Olivia."

"No." I shake my head. "He's not that hot."

"Get your eyes checked."

"He called my office today when I was in a meeting." I sigh as I exit Alexander's website and drop my phone back into my oversized black leather tote. "He left a message with Sheryl."

"Oh, poor you." She smirks. "You returned his call, didn't you?"

By the time my assistant, Sheryl, gave me the message it was almost six o'clock. I promised Kate that I'd be at her store at six, so I left my office with the intention of calling Alexander back tomorrow.

"I didn't have time."

She glances at the silver watch on her wrist. "According to this, you have all the time in the world."

I playfully pat her hand. "I'll call him when I get to my office in the morning. I thought we were going for pizza."

In one swift movement, she's clutching my hand in hers. "You're interested in him, aren't you?"

I almost laugh. "Who?"

"Alexander." She points a finger at me. "That's why you're putting off calling him back. You're trying to figure out what you'll say to him."

I suck in a deep breath. That's not why I'm putting off

calling him back. "I swore off all arrogant and cocky men years ago. He's attractive, but he's not my type, Kate."

"She who protests too much…" Her voice trails.

"I'll call him tomorrow," I repeat as I gaze around her store and the potential customers checking out the dresses and accessories. "Are you sure you can pull yourself away for a dinner break?"

"My staff can handle it." She straightens the collar of the red dress she's wearing. "I've been craving pizza all day. I'm ordering a huge slice of pepperoni. How about you?"

Pizza isn't my favorite, but spending time with Kate ranks high on my list of things I love to do. "I'm having the same."

"Let's go." She takes off toward the door of the shop. "I've only got an hour to spare. Try to keep up."

I laugh as I fall in step behind her.

CHAPTER SEVEN

ALEXANDER

OLIVIA HULL.

That's her standing next to Trey Hale in a picture he posted to his Instagram account last year.

The caption says it all: *Best Cousin Ever!*

The photo was liked more than a half million times and the comments number in the thousands.

They're both dressed in jeans, matching baseball jerseys and Yankees ball caps.

Olivia's is skewed to the side to reveal her entire face.

It's beautiful. Her smile is infectious.

Dammit. She's a gorgeous woman.

She's also compassionate.

I'm grateful that she went to her cousin so that I wouldn't walk into Alvin's birthday party empty-handed.

I'm slightly pissed that she didn't return my call yesterday.

After I discovered her connection to Trey on his Instagram account, I pulled up the Liore Lingerie corporate site and zeroed in on her bio page.

Another breathtaking image of her greeted me. In that one, she was dressed in a white blouse and blue blazer. The fuck-me red lipstick she had on piqued my interest.

It gave her an edgy look that stirred my cock.

I don't know if my driving desire to talk to the woman is born from my thankfulness over what she did for my nephew or my attraction to her.

"That's a cute picture of Olivia you have there."

I look up from my phone and into the face of Olivia's assistant, Sheryl. The woman is efficient. When she left me standing here, in front of her desk, I expected her to be gone for more than two minutes.

"Did you find Olivia?" I ask abruptly as I slide my phone into the pocket of my suit jacket. "Did you tell her that I'm waiting to speak to her?"

"That would be a no and a no, Mr. Donato." She sighs heavily. "Ms. Hull's meeting ended more than an hour ago. She must have left the building for lunch."

I drop my gaze to the flowers in my hand. I want to show my gratitude for what she did for Alvin. I didn't bother with a card when I stopped by the florist to pick up the large bouquet. I assumed I'd be handing the flowers to Olivia in person, along with my words of appreciation.

"Are those for her?" Sheryl reaches for the bouquet.

I pull them closer to me. "Can you call her and find out when she'll be back?"

"I guess I can if that's what you want." She tosses me a puzzled look before she rounds her desk and picks up a cell phone. "I'm glad to see she's dating someone like you. The last man she was with wasn't her type at all."

"We're not…" I begin before I'm stopped by the rise of her hand in the air.

"Olivia?" She asks into the phone before she pauses. "Your boyfriend is here at the office to see you."

She sighs and lets out a small chuckle. "Alexander Donato."

Sheryl's eyes rake me over as she listens intently. "He's not? Oh. I'm sorry. I just assumed. It's been a long time since you…"

I clear my throat as she stops again to listen.

"He wants to speak with you." Her gaze drops to the top of her desk. "All right. I'll tell him."

She lowers the phone from her ear and studies the screen. It fades to black under her gaze.

I wait for her to say something, anything, but she continues to stare at her phone silently.

I clear my throat. "When will she be back?"

That prompts a slow raise of her chin until her eyes meet mine. "She won't be back in the office today. She was called into one of our retail locations to handle a problem that popped up."

"Which location?" I ask. "I'll head over there to speak to her."

She looks at the flowers again. "She's very busy today. She said that you could expect a call from her tomorrow once she's back in her office."

"I'd like to talk to her today," I press. "It's an urgent matter, Sheryl."

"She didn't mention that," she mutters under her breath. "Is this business or personal? Olivia didn't get into any detail on the phone."

I see the unmistakable glint of curiosity in her eyes. The

woman is dying to know what my connection to Olivia is and what the flowers symbolize.

I use her nosiness to my advantage. "It's a personal matter. The flowers are a surprise. Thank you for not mentioning them to her during the call. I can't wait to see the expression on her face when she sees them."

She reaches out to touch my arm. "Olivia didn't specifically say that I couldn't tell you where she is. You won't take up too much of her time, will you?"

I place my hand over hers. "Five minutes, Sheryl. I just want five minutes to hand her the flowers and see the smile on her face."

She heaves a breathy sigh. "She's at the Liore boutique in Tribeca."

"I'll make my way over there now." I take a few steps before I turn back. "Let's keep this between us. I want Olivia to be shocked when I walk in."

"I won't say a word." She shakes her head. " Ms. Hull doesn't have enough romance in her life. I'm not going to ruin this for her."

CHAPTER EIGHT

Olivia

I SHOULD FIRE SHERYL.

"Mr. Donato," I whisper his name. "What are you doing here?"

He stares at me. "I came to thank you."

I skim my hands over the wrinkled skirt of my red dress. My hair is a mess. I've spent the better part of the last thirty minutes in the stock room rummaging through a box of satin boy shorts that were sent to this store by mistake.

The shipment was destined for our competitor who just opened a new location a block from here.

Trying to locate the purchase order that was tucked into the box with the hundreds of pair of underwear wasn't an easy task.

The manager of this store called me in a panic right before lunch because she assumed this shipment was part of our winter line and she had no record of the order.

She wanted to know the unit number for the shorts in our point of sale software program.

I couldn't find it so I told her I'd come down to sort things out.

I asked her repeatedly if the box was addressed to this Liore location. She assured me it was.

I didn't realize until I looked at the shipping label that the delivery person is the one who made a mistake.

"These are for you." Alexander pushes a large bunch of flowers toward me. "Thank you for what you did for my nephew."

I brush the bouquet away with a swat of my hand. "This isn't necessary."

A gasp from a woman standing near us turns both our heads. "How ungrateful," she mutters under her breath.

"It is necessary." Alexander shifts his gaze back to my face. "You did something special for my nephew. I appreciate that."

My first instinct is to deny that I'm the person responsible for the replacement jersey for his nephew, but he's so sure of himself. Buck must have let it slip that I'm the one who went to Trey.

"You should thank Buck, not me." I glance around the boutique and the dozen or so customers who are now staring at the two of us. I drop my voice to barely more than a whisper. "He's the one who broke his promise to me."

Alexander's gaze follows mine. "Is there somewhere more private that we can talk?"

I run a hand through my hair. "There's an office in the back. We can talk there."

I lead the way, feeling every set of eyes in the boutique following each move we make.

———

"DON'T BLAME BUCK," Alexander says as I close the door of the office. He turns his phone screen toward me.

I stare at the picture of Trey and me in matching baseball jerseys and caps.

Dammit.

I remember the day that picture was taken. It was last spring, and we were having lunch in Boston on Mother's Day.

Trey thought our moms would get a kick out of the two of us dressing alike.

They did.

My mom was the one who took the photo using Trey's phone. He sent it to me, but I had no idea that he also uploaded it to his Instagram account.

"The only clue he gave me was that a female relative of Trey's told him about my stolen jersey." He shoves the phone back into the pocket of his gray dress slacks.

He's wearing black shoes and a black V-neck sweater.

His dark hair is tousled in that sexy way that only men who look like him can pull off.

Get a grip, Olivia. He's not your type.

Since I'm standing in silence, he goes on. "I thought it was a long shot when I started going through Trey's old Instagram posts, but I struck gold when I found that picture of the two of you."

I tug on one of my earrings, suddenly feeling self-conscious about how I looked in the picture and how I look now. "You didn't have to come all the way down here to thank me."

He pushes the flowers toward me again. "I wanted to give you these to thank you for what you did for Alvin."

"Alvin?" I repeat the name back. "Is that your nephew?"

His phone is in his palm again. He shows me the screen and an image of a young blond haired boy with big blue eyes. "He's my sister's kid. Your cousin is his hero."

Any lingering reservations I had about going to Trey to ask for a signed jersey, disappear at the sight of that boy's smiling face. "I'm glad I could help."

"You did more than help." He stares intently into my eyes. "Alvin is going to meet Trey. He's going to watch the first game of the World Series from one of the best seats in the house and that's all because of you."

"Trey loves his fans." I try to shift the focus of his gratitude to my cousin. All I did was ask for a jersey. "Trey and his agent came up with the idea for the game tickets and the meeting. I can't take any credit for that."

"You're the one who got the ball rolling." He moves the flowers closer to me. "Please accept these as a small token of my appreciation."

I begrudgingly reach for the bouquet, knowing that every employee in this boutique is going to question me about the flowers and the handsome man who gave them to me.

I clear my throat. "Thank you. They're lovely."

"Have dinner with me."

Dumbfounded, I fumble with something to say. I didn't expect a dinner invitation. Hell, I didn't expect him to come down to the boutique today. "No...I won't...I mean, I can't..."

If he's offended, it's hidden behind the brilliant smile on his face. "You can't or you won't. Which is it?"

"It's not necessary," I clarify, not wanting to look like a fool because I instantly assumed that the invitation was for a date, not a *thanks-for-making-my-nephew's-dreams-come-true* dinner. "The flowers are thank you enough."

Confusion knits his brow. "The flowers are a start."

"They're enough," I argue.

"Hardly," he spits back. "I'll be in touch, Ms. Hull."

"Why?" I ask as he starts toward the office door. "I did you a favor. You thanked me. That's the end."

"I'm in your debt." He stops to look me over. "I always repay my debts."

Before I can say anything else, he turns on his heel, opens the door and disappears into the crowded boutique, turning every female head he passes.

I have no idea what the hell just happened between Alexander and me but he's wrong, he doesn't owe me a thing.

CHAPTER NINE

ALEXANDER

"I DON'T EVEN CARE that they lost," Alvin says through a laugh. "This was the best night of my life, Alex."

It ranks up there with one of the best of mine too.

When I told him yesterday, at his birthday party, that we'd be spending a good part of Sunday night cheering on his favorite team from the stands, his face lit up.

The tears started when I added that he'd be meeting Trey Hale.

Phoebe told me that he didn't sleep a wink last night. I can see that in his face now.

He's crashing hard from the excitement of this weekend and that unforgettable moment when he hugged his hero.

Trey couldn't have been any more gracious.

"You ready to head home?" I ask as I pick up the team jacket, pennants and ball that Buck handed us when he brought us to our seats after the meet and greet.

Alvin has been wearing the autographed jersey since Trey presented it to him under a barrage of camera flashes.

Phoebe was fine with Alvin's face being plastered all over social media and television. She signed the release form Buck forwarded to me without question.

I only wish I could have brought her along to witness this.

I look out at the emptying stadium and the star-dotted sky.

Life is good. It's so damn good right now.

"I want to stay here forever." Alvin's hand reaches for mine. "I've never been to a game before. Do you think we can come back sometime?"

I look down at the sight of his small hand in mine. "You bet. I can't promise the same treatment next time, but we'll…"

"I can."

Alvin's head snaps back at the sound of Trey Hale's voice behind us.

I turn to see him, still dressed in his uniform, standing next to Buck.

"Trey." Alvin rushes toward him but stops a foot short of him. "Good job out there tonight."

Trey's expression softens as he tugs the ball cap from his head and places it on Alvin's. "We'll do even better next game."

Alvin's fingers skim the brim of the cap. "I'll be watching with my mom at home. She's a big fan too, but she doesn't know all the stats the way I do."

"Those two seats are empty for tomorrow night's game." Buck motions to the seats Alvin and I occupied. "You think your mom would want to bring you back to watch Trey win?"

"Hey now." Trey elbows him. "Let's rephrase that. Do you think your mom could bring you tomorrow to watch us play our hearts out?"

Alvin scratches his cheek as he turns to look at me. "What do you think, Alex? If mom can't bring me, will you?"

"Your mom will make the time," I say without any doubt in my voice. I know my sister. She'll jump at the chance to sit next to her son tomorrow night. "We'll tell her about it as soon as we get to your place."

"I'll have two passes waiting for them at the box office," Buck says before looking down at my nephew. "Do you need another soda to take with you for the ride home? Maybe a candy bar?"

"Yes, please." Alvin's voice vibrates with excitement.

"Let's go pick something from the concession stand before they close it up for the night." Buck glances at me. "There's a car waiting to take you back to Queens."

"Thanks, Buck." I smile when I spot the look of pure contentment on Alvin's face. "I'll be right there, Alvin."

"I'm not in a hurry." He turns his attention to Trey. "Maybe I'll see you around?"

"You know it." Trey pats his shoulder before Alvin takes off on Buck's heel.

I move toward Trey with my hand outstretched. "I can't thank you enough for everything you've done. As you can see, you've not only made Alvin's night, you've made his life."

He lets out a laugh as he gives my hand a firm shake. "I was his age once. I loved the game too. I know what it means to sit in these stands."

What he's given to Alvin can't be measured on any scale. We both know it. I don't need to explain that to him. "I'll have to thank Olivia again for her part in this."

"You know about that?" Trey crosses his arms over his chest. "Did Buck fuck up and let it slip?"

I chuckle with a shake of my head. "He only gave me a

clue. He said it was a female relative. I pieced the rest together myself."

"Olivia knows that you know?" His brows lift.

"I gave her flowers last week to thank her." I'm mildly surprised that he didn't hear about that, although I have no idea how close they are.

I wouldn't know any of my cousins if I passed them on the street. My family is separated, not only by physical distance but emotional vastness.

"Good." He jerks his chin. "She's a great person. She's always looking out for everyone else. I'm glad to hear that you took the time to send her flowers."

"I hand delivered them." I glance over his shoulder to where Buck is standing next to Alvin. "She was working at one of the boutiques that day."

"Working too hard, no doubt." He steals a glance behind him. "Olivia's the hardest working person I know. I'm surprised she showed up tonight."

"Olivia was here?"

"Front row." He gestures to the field. "She always comes out to the first home games of the season and the series if we make it. It's tradition."

I want to ask if she came with someone, but her relationship status is none of my business. I hadn't even considered it until this point.

Maybe that's why she had such a strong reaction to my question about dinner. She's involved with someone.

I glance over at Alvin again. "I should go. I need to get my nephew back home before the stroke of midnight, or my sister will never forgive me."

Trey laughs. "It was good to meet you, Alex. Maybe we'll run into each other again."

"You bet," I say as I brush past him.

Something tells me that this won't be the last time I see Trey Hale.

CHAPTER TEN

OLIVIA

I WATCH as another flower petal drops onto my desk. The bouquet that Alexander gave me almost two weeks ago isn't technically a bouquet anymore. It's a bunch of stems with withering petals in a tall vase sitting in an inch of yellowed water.

It's a testament to how often I receive flowers.

I'm holding onto these until the very last petal has fallen and the stems have dried up. Only then, will I let Sheryl take the vase away.

She pokes her head into my office in another attempt to wrestle the dying flowers from my grasp. "Are you sure you don't want me to dump that vase, Olivia?"

"No." I look over a blank piece of paper in front of me. "When the time is right, I'll take care of it."

She sighs. "I can stop by the market on my way to work tomorrow and pick up a fresh bouquet. Consider it my treat to you."

Is that pity in her green eyes?

The only flowers that are ever delivered to the office for me are on my birthday and those are from my mom.

The card bears the same message every year.

To my daughter on her birthday.

Love, your mother.

My mom loves me more than anything, but heartfelt messages are not her way of showing it.

"You don't have to do that." I lean back in my chair. "I appreciate the thought."

"Cathleen stopped by earlier looking for you." Sheryl straightens and takes a step into my office. "She said it wasn't urgent."

If my boss wants to talk to me, that takes precedence over everything else.

Cathleen Dickerson is the person who gave me this job. She was the one who encouraged me to pursue a degree in business and once I earned it, she promoted me by making me her junior assistant.

I've worked up the ranks since then, always with her encouragement and support.

"She didn't say what it was about?" I ask for clarification since Sheryl isn't quick to offer every small detail of her exchanges with other staff.

"Nope." She moves closer to my desk. "I'll call her and ask if she has a minute to see you now."

I push back from my desk and stand. "I'll run up to her office and see if she's around."

Sheryl gives me the once-over. "I love that pencil skirt on you, Olivia."

I glance down at the black pencil skirt and white blouse I'm wearing. It's my go-to outfit whenever I can't decide what to wear. "Thanks, Sheryl."

"Do you need me to take care of anything while you're gone?" She points at the dying flowers.

"No." I usher her out of my office with a brush of my hand against her elbow. "You can email Steph about the new bra line that's launching in the spring. Tell her I'll drop by with samples later this week."

"That I can do." Sheryl turns to look at me. "Have I told you lately what a great boss you are?"

"Twice today, but I'm listening." I laugh as I start down the corridor toward the elevator. "By the way, you're an amazing assistant, Sheryl. I'll be back right away."

"Take your time," she calls after me. "Have fun up there with the big shots."

I laugh even though I hope one day, I'll have an office on the top floor of this building.

———

LOWERING myself into one of the chairs facing Cathleen's desk, I wait while she shuts her office door.

My heart is thumping out a beat that I can feel in my toes even though I know I haven't done anything to warrant a warning. The smile on Cathleen's face when she saw me approaching her office was reassuring.

She ushered me past her assistant without a word.

"Sheryl told me that you stopped by my office," I finally speak as she rounds her desk to take her chair. "I thought I'd come up and see what you needed."

"Two tickets to Alexander Donato's opening night."

"What?" My eyes widen as my pulse picks up even more. "I think I misheard you."

"You didn't." She leans back in her chair. "From what

I've heard, the man has been following you around Manhattan."

If he has, he's damn good at hiding it. I haven't seen him since the day he popped into the boutique in Tribeca and handed me the flowers.

"I'm not sure what you mean," I say genuinely, wondering if this is indeed what she came down to my office to talk about. If it is, I'm disappointed. I was hoping it was about my stellar work.

"I'm joking, Olivia." Her lips smooth into a smile. "I heard that he was in the building looking for you a couple of weeks ago before he showed up at the Tribeca boutique."

"I helped him with something," I offer. "He just wanted to thank me."

"He was here earlier." She glances at the closed door of her office. "He spent some time with Gabriel."

Gabriel Foster. He's the man in charge.

He's the CEO of Foster Enterprises. His family owns Liore Lingerie, as well as several other clothing companies.

He knows me by name, but we've never had a conversation beyond a short one about the weather in the elevator.

"He came here to see Mr. Foster?" I question in an effort to gain even an ounce of understanding about what Alexander is up to.

"Gabriel's wife is the second principal violinist with the Philharmonic."

I didn't know that.

"So Alexander was here to talk about Mrs. Foster?" I clench my teeth. I'm sliding into territory that I don't belong.

It doesn't matter why Alexander was here. It shouldn't be piquing my curiosity as much as it is.

"Gabriel wanted to offer his assistance in the event that

Alexander needed anything." She bows her head. "You know how gracious he is."

Not really.

"Gabriel told me that your name came up and Alexander had only complimentary things to say. He told Gabriel that you helped him out of a difficult situation after he walked into the store on Fifth Avenue. I believe his exact words were that 'Olivia Hull went above and beyond the call of duty.' Gabriel is impressed."

That's a point for me in my quest to land an office on this floor one day.

"I'm glad I could help."

Cathleen pushes to stand. I follow suit because I know it's a sign that she's moving on to the next thing on her to-do list for today.

"There's one other thing, Olivia."

"What's that?"

"A position in the corporate office in London is opening up." Her eyes lock on mine. "Your name has come up."

No freaking way.

I know exactly what job she's talking about.

Regional Director of Operations.

It's a step up from what I'm doing now and it entails all of our European locations.

"You're open to relocating, aren't you?"

I nod. I don't have any ties to New York City other than Trey and a handful of friends. I know that he'd love to visit me in London. Kate would too and my mom has always talked about going on a European vacation. This would be her chance to do that as often as she likes.

"We're going to send out an interest form to everyone who is qualified within the next few weeks." She looks down at the large calendar on her desk. "I'm encouraging you to seriously consider throwing your hat into this ring."

I know it's not a firm offer, but I take her words at face value. She believes I have a chance to land the job.

"I will." My mouth curves into a smile.

"Good. I trust you'll keep this to yourself for now." She taps her hand on her desk. "I've got a meeting to get to. I'm glad you stopped by."

I am too.

It may not be an office on this floor, but it's just as good. It's London.

I never imagined that was within my grasp. Cathleen just showed me that my dream is closer than I ever thought it was.

CHAPTER ELEVEN

ALEXANDER

"SEND a pair of tickets to Trey Hale and a pair to his agent Buck Remsen. Also, I want two sent to Olivia Hull." I glance out the window of my apartment at the rain pelting Manhattan. "I've sent you an email with all of their contact information. Invite each to the reception after the performance."

I end the call with Vito, my manager, before he can get in another word.

He's already talking about my next venture. According to him, I should accept an offer to guest conduct in Australia early next year.

I'm not feeling the pull that I usually do when a new opportunity crosses my path.

My connection to Alvin is growing day-by-day. We spent hours talking about the World Series and I was his first call when it was over.

I could hear Phoebe in the background cheering, but

Alvin's voice broke when he told me he was proud of Trey and his teammates for winning the series. The kid's birthday gift sparked a new connection for us.

I'm still just Alex to him, but I don't care. I'm finding a spot in his life that I can fill and that's good enough for me.

"I don't get to see you on opening night?" Jack walks into the main living space with two beers in his hands. He shoves one at me. "I'm not a hometown hero like Trey Hale, and my name isn't as cool as Buck Remsen, but I thought I'd score a set of tickets."

"Go to hell," I joke. "I had two sent to your office yesterday."

"That's what was in that envelope?" He drops onto my leather couch. "I should pay more attention when I get a delivery from you."

"Who are you bringing?" I take a pull from the beer.

Jack brought six bottles over. It's good. I don't drink often, but when Jack and I get together, a bottle of imported is usually in each of our hands.

"I haven't decided yet," he mutters. "I'll surprise you."

I move to sit on the chair opposite him. "You're coming solo, aren't you?"

"And waste a ticket?" He shakes his head. "No way in hell. I'm still considering my options."

"Bring your assistant."

"Everly?" He huffs out a laugh. "She doesn't strike me as the symphony type, Alex."

She's his type, even if he can't see it.

"Forget about Everly. Let's talk about Olivia Hull." He places the beer on the wooden coffee table in front of him. "Who is she?"

I follow suit and put mine down too. "Trey's cousin."

"Ah." He leans back on the couch. "So she's the one who came to your rescue when your one-night stand fucked off with the autographed jersey?"

"That's her." I nod. "She went to Trey, his agent got involved and the rest is history."

"So the tickets are just your way of saying thank you to her?"

I shrug. "I gave her flowers. The tickets are another way to thank her."

He sets one ankle on the opposite knee. His gray suit is expensive, his shoes more so. It looks like handling my money is paying off for him. Although, I'm only one of the dozens of clients he has.

"You're interested in this woman, aren't you?" He reaches forward to grab his beer.

"She's interesting," I counter. "She's not impressed by who I am."

"You make it sound like that's rare." He laughs. "Do women fall at your feet when they realize you're *the* Alexander Donato?"

They do. More often than he'd realize.

"Olivia is a good person." The words leave my mouth before I think them through. "She did me a huge favor. I don't think a lot of women in this city would be willing to go to that much trouble to help a stranger."

"You don't think she did it because of who you are?" He tips his bottle toward me. "Maybe she's looking for a hook-up with the master conductor."

If she is, she's doing a hell of a good job playing hard to get.

"She did it for Alvin." I glance down at the screen of my phone when it chimes. "The pasta I ordered is here."

"It's about time." He finishes what's left in the bottle in his hand. "I'll grab us another beer."

———

TREY: **Hey Alex! I got the tickets. I'll be there. Thanks, man!**

I smile at the text message.

It's been days since Vito send out the ticket packages to Trey, Buck and Olivia.

Buck called me the next day to thank me for the invitation. He's bringing his ex-wife in an attempt to rekindle the fire.

If I can play a part in a reunion, I'm happy to oblige.

I type out a response to Trey.

Alexander: **I'll see you then.**

My fingers hover over the screen. I'm tempted to ask about Olivia. I haven't heard anything from her since the tickets were delivered to her office. I have no idea if she's even a fan of the symphony.

I press send as the sound of elevator doors opening draws my gaze up.

"Mr. Donato?"

I look her over. She's wearing a pale pink skirt and a sheer black blouse. Her hair is pulled back into a messy knot at the base of her neck.

Olivia Hull has to be the most beautiful woman I've ever met.

"Olivia," I greet her as she takes a step off the elevator. "It's good to see you."

She adjusts the black trench coat slung over her forearm as she looks around the lobby of the Foster Enterprises building. "What are you doing here?"

I could lie and say that I'm here to see her, but I doubt that would earn me a smile.

I can't tell if she's as attracted to me as I am to her. The puzzled look on her face at the moment isn't helping.

"I'm here to see Gabriel Foster." I watch as the elevator doors slide shut. "We're meeting for lunch."

She nods, her teeth tugging on the corner of her bottom lip. "I need to go. I have to be uptown in ten minutes."

"Did you get the tickets to the symphony and the invitation to the reception?" I ask casually as she turns to walk away.

Her eyes scan my face. "I did. It wasn't necessary, but thank you."

"You'll come?"

A blush blooms high on her cheeks. If I knew her mind was going to wander there, I wouldn't have phrased it as a question.

She'd come with me. I'd make it my mission every time I fucked her.

Her hand darts to her cheek, her fingers feathering a path over her smooth skin. "I'm not sure. I have to check my schedule. I think I may have plans for that night."

My gaze glides over her left hand.

No ring.

She's not married or engaged.

If there's a boyfriend, I'll back off.

I fish for more. "If you do have plans, perhaps you and your boyfriend could at least make time for the performance. I promise it will be a night to remember."

She takes a deep breath. "I'll have a closer look at my schedule. I do need to run now, Mr. Donato."

"Alexander."

"Alexander," she repeats back softly. "Goodbye."

I don't respond.

I watch her walk away, wondering if another man is going to have her in his bed tonight.

If that's the case, I hate the lucky son-of-a-bitch.

CHAPTER TWELVE

OLIVIA

"HYPOTHETICALLY SPEAKING..." I trail my words. Looking in Kate's direction, I smile while I wait for her response.

"Olivia." She reaches for a lace veil before she turns to face me. "Don't. Just tell me what it is. I already know it's about you."

"And you," I counter as I smooth my hand over the long train of a bridal gown.

I met Kate here at her store, Katie Rose Bridal, after I was done work. She's still on the clock. Her mission at the moment is to select dresses and veils for a celebrity bride-to-be who has a consultation booked with her tomorrow morning.

"Me?" She hangs the veil on the silver garment rack that she's been wheeling around the store. "How does this involve me?"

"Do you like the symphony?" I ask with a wide grin.

"I like that pink skirt you have on." She laughs as she looks down at the black jumpsuit she's wearing. "Can I borrow it sometime?"

She already knows the answer to that question. We've been passing clothing items back and forth between our apartments for the last few months. Sometimes when I get dressed in the morning, I'm not even sure if the clothes I'm putting on belong to her or me.

"Anytime."

"*Thank you*," she mouths.

"The symphony, Kate." I glance at an off-white wedding dress that's covered with feathers. "Do you like it?"

"I've never been. I'm not sure if I like it or not," she confesses with a wink. "Is this related to Alexander Donato?"

My eyes widen. "You've never been to the symphony?"

"Nice try, Liv." She picks up a crown veil and holds it in the air, examining it from all angles. "Don't skip over my question about Alexander. Is this conversation about him or not?"

I move to where she's standing and run my fingers over the edge of a vintage veil that's been embroidered with crystals. "He sent me two tickets to his first performance and an invitation to the reception after the show."

Her gaze darts to my face. "We're going. No question."

"No question? You've made up your mind?"

She picks up the veil I've been admiring. "This is perfect. Why didn't I notice this one?"

I shrug. "I haven't decided if I want to go to the symphony."

"No." Her voice is firm. "You haven't decided if you like Alexander or not. I think you do, but that's not the point."

I can't hold back a small laugh. "What's the point?"

"The point is that we have an opportunity to go to the

symphony and to what will probably be a fancy ass reception afterward. How can we turn that down?" A smile spreads across her face. "It's way better than another night of Netflix and popcorn. It's an adventure for the two of us, so let's do it. What is there to lose?"

My heart.

I have no idea why that thought crossed my mind.

I'm not going to lose my heart at the symphony. I may lose a couple of hours of my life, but that's the only risk I see.

"Once I'm done here we can go back to your place and choose dresses to wear." She claps her hands together.

"My place?" I laugh.

"You must own at least twenty little black dresses." She rests a hand on my shoulder. "We'll pick dresses from your closet, and accessories from mine."

"Deal," I say, dropping into a chair. "I'll sit and wait patiently until you're done your work, Katie Rose."

She turns back toward the rack of wedding dresses. "One day I'll be doing this for you. I'll find the perfect wedding dress when you're ready to make it official with the man of your dreams."

"Slow down." I cross my legs and lean back in the chair. "Give me a chance to meet him first.'"

Glancing over her shoulder, she winks at me. "Maybe you already have."

I point at my watch. "If you can get this done in the next thirty minutes, I'll buy us both dinner before we go shopping in my closet."

"Challenge accepted." She laughs. "We'll be out of this place in fifteen. You know I can't resist free food."

———

"IT LOOKS like the gang's all here," Kate says as she slips her leather jacket from her shoulders. "Is he the reason why you wanted to come to this pub?"

"Trey?" I ask with a straight face. "I had no idea my cousin would be here."

It's the truth.

I also didn't have a clue that Alexander Donato would be sitting next to him at the bar.

They haven't noticed us yet and for that I'm grateful. All I wanted was a bowl of clam chowder. Easton Pub makes the best in the city, but I've suddenly lost my appetite.

"I'm not talking about Trey." She folds her jacket over the back of a chair next to a wooden table. "I'm talking about the conductor."

"Let's go." I grab her jacket. "There's a great sushi place by our building. I think you'll like it."

"I'd like a bowl of chowder." She plops herself down on the chair. "It looks like Trey and Alexander are deep in discussion so you can wipe that look of panic off of your face."

I laugh, even though I know I look stressed. I didn't plan on running into Alexander twice in one day.

When I left him standing in the lobby next to the bank of elevators hours ago, I felt flushed. The man does something to me even if I'm not ready to admit it to myself.

I fold both of our coats over the back of my chair before I take a seat.

A female server approaches with two menus in her hands. "Good evening, ladies. I'm Kora. Welcome to Easton Pub."

Kate smiles up at the pretty brunette. "Please tell me that you have clam chowder tonight."

"Every night." Kora holds the menus in the air. "Are you going to need these or is it chowder for the both of you?"

"Chowder and two glasses of water with lemon." Kate looks at me. "Unless you want something stronger, Liv."

I shake my head while I try to keep my gaze focused on her and not the movement at the bar that I'm catching out of the corner of my eye. "Water is fine."

Kora leaves in a rush, headed straight toward the kitchen.

The distinctive smell of chowder fills the air around us.

I first fell in love with this place when Trey asked me to meet him here for lunch last winter. I wasn't a seafood fan before that snowy day, but I converted as soon as I had my first taste.

I'm not surprised that he's here. It's one of his favorite places to eat.

"Alexander, Trey and some super hot guy in a suit are headed in this direction." Kate's gaze wanders toward the bar before it settles back on my face. "Things are about to get interesting."

CHAPTER THIRTEEN

ALEXANDER

I DIDN'T EXPECT to see Olivia tonight.

When Jack suggested we meet at Easton Pub for dinner, I was on board.

After my lunch with Gabriel, I spent the afternoon working. Readying for my tenure as the conductor of the Philharmonic is stressful, but satisfying.

I'm confident that I'll be in sync with not only the orchestra but also the audience when I take the stage.

"I can't believe I ran into Alexander and you here." Trey squeezes Olivia's shoulder, drawing her gaze to his face. "The chowder is irresistible, isn't it?"

Her eyes shift from Trey to me. "You know how much I love it."

"Jack Pearce." Jack's hand darts past me as he extends it toward Olivia. "I've heard only good things about you from these two, Ms. Hull."

"I prefer Olivia." She takes his hand for a light shake. "It's nice to meet you."

"I'm Kate Wesley." The pretty blonde who arrived with Olivia shoves her hand into Jack's. "Olivia and I are friends. We live in the same building."

"This is Alexander Donato." Jack elbows me. "He's usually not this quiet."

Everyone but Olivia laughs.

"I'm heading out." Trey moves to kiss Olivia on the forehead. "I'm flying to Hawaii in a couple of weeks. You're welcome to tag along, Livi."

Livi.

A blush creeps up her cheeks as she taps him on the hand. "I have to work, but give them both a kiss for me."

Trey straightens and turns to face Jack and I. "Our moms are sisters. They hang out in Maui when the temperature dips in the northeast."

He's a good guy. That's evident in the way he speaks of his family. I spent the last hour listening to him talk about his two older brothers and his late father.

It gave me insight into the man he is. He's also an uncle, and from what I'm learning now a devoted son and cousin.

"It was good to meet you, Trey." Jack shoves his hand into the inner pocket of his suit jacket and pulls out a business card. "Let's meet up for a beer once you're back on the mainland."

I'm not surprised by the suggestion.

Jack is always on the hunt for new clients and Trey would be the ultimate.

"I'll drop you a text when I'm back." Trey takes the card and heads for the door.

I glance down at Olivia. Her eyes are pinned to her friend.

Again, I have no fucking idea if she's happy to see me or if she wishes I'd go straight to hell.

She's a hard read.

"Do you want to join us?" Kate asks with a smirk. "We ordered the chowder, but I can flag down the server and get her to bring two more bowls."

"We actually just…"

Ate is the word about to leave Jack's mouth, but I stop it with a hard bump of my shoulder against his.

"We'd love to." I pull out the empty chair next to Olivia and sit. "I've never had the chowder here. Is it good?"

Jack huffs out a laugh as he slides into the chair opposite me. "I had it very recently and it was incredible, Alex."

I respond with a raised brow and a scowl.

I don't give a shit that he ate two bowls while we sat at the bar talking to Trey. I'm full from the club sandwich I downed in record time.

Olivia Hull is a mystery to me and I want to know more.

I watch her as her gaze travels the room before it lands on me.

"Olivia and I are excited about the symphony." Kate rests her elbows on the table. "We're both looking forward to it and the reception too."

"You decided to come?" I turn and look at Olivia's profile. "And you're bringing Kate?"

She nods but doesn't say a word.

If there's a man in her life, he's failing miserably at being available for her.

"Hello again." Kora's distinctive voice rises above the background noise as she approaches.

She's been our very attentive server all night, even though we tried to order food from the bartender. He called her over to take care of that. It paid off for her.

Jack tipped her well when he closed our tab.

"We're going to need two more bowls of clam chowder," Kate says. "What are you two drinking?"

"More clam chowder?" Kora eyes Jack. "You're sure about that?"

"You heard the woman." Jack smirks. "Chowder and four beers. The night is young."

"We have plans after dinner," Olivia blurts out. "Kate and I made plans."

Kate's brow furrows as she looks across the table at her friend. "We're not in a rush, Liv. Let's enjoy our dinner and the company."

She's a wise woman.

I plan on enjoying every moment of this dinner. I haven't spent more than a few minutes with Olivia, but there's something about her that makes me want to know more.

———

"I'M DONE." Kate pushes her bowl away from her. "If I eat another bite I won't fit into the dress I'm planning on wearing to the symphony."

A smile spreads across Olivia's mouth. "Didn't we have plans to pick out dresses tonight, Kate?"

Kate's gaze falls to her phone. "We did, but I have to stop at the boutique first. I'll meet up with you in an hour at your place."

A rise of her shoulders and a soft sigh are the only reply from Olivia.

"No rest for the weary." Jack pushes back from the table. "I need to meet a client to go over something pressing."

I predicted as much when I noticed him texting non-stop

during our second dinner. Jack is respectful enough to put his phone away unless it's an emergency.

This must fall into that category.

"It was great meeting you both." Jack stands. "Enjoy the rest of your evening."

"It was good meeting you too," Olivia calls after him.

"Thank you again for dinner, Alexander." Kate reaches for her purse. "I'll be at your place in an hour, Olivia."

Olivia nods as her friend gets up and walks away leaving the two of us alone.

CHAPTER FOURTEEN

Olivia

HOW IN THE hell did I end up alone with Alexander and why are my palms so sweaty?

I grip the paper napkin in my fist even tighter.

I'm a bundle of nerves for some reason.

Usually, I'm fine around men. There have been times in the past when I've put my foot in my mouth, or I've spilled food on my dress, but tonight I kept it together on the outside, even though I feel like I'm riding a rollercoaster on the inside.

Alexander Donato smells incredible.

If I could spray that cologne on my pillow each night, I'd fall asleep with a smile on my face.

Maybe it's not cologne; maybe he smells this good on his own.

His hands fall to his jean covered thighs.

"Olivia," he says my name and I feel like I just dropped into a curve on the roller coaster.

My heartbeat speeds. My breathing stalls.

"Yes?"

"Can I buy you a drink? Perhaps a brandy?"

I glance at his face. It's gorgeous. His jaw is covered in late day stubble and he's rocking that bad boy, messy hair look.

The dark sweater he's wearing only adds to the allure.

Why do the arrogant ones always have to be this hot?

"I need to get home." I pick up my phone.

"Why?"

"Why?" I repeat back as I tap a finger on my phone's screen. "I live there, so that's where I go at the end of the day."

He laughs. It's not a muted chuckle. It's full-on throwing-his-head-back-laughter.

I look back to my phone as the laughter fades.

"Kate said she wouldn't be meeting you there for an hour," he points out. "You have time for a drink."

"I appreciate the offer, but I should go." I shake my phone in the air in exasperation. "Dammit."

"What's wrong?" He leans closer to me.

"The battery must have died. I forgot to charge it earlier." I push back from the table, suddenly feeling as though there's not enough air in the room. "I need to get an Uber."

He's on his feet before I am, his hand resting on the back of my chair. "I'll call the car service I use. They'll send a driver right over for us."

"Us?" I parrot back, blowing out a deep breath. I reach for my bag and toss my useless phone inside. "I can get home on my own. I'll flag down a cab outside."

I start toward the door, aware that's he's on my heel.

"Olivia, wait," he calls as my hand hits handle of the door. "You forgot your coat."

Of course I did. I'm flustered from seeing him tonight and his suggestion to share a ride.

I don't know if the man thinks I'll invite him up to my apartment. He knows that I'm expecting Kate soon so unless he fucks fast, he's not trying to get into my panties.

He strikes me as the kind of man that takes his time in bed.

Jesus, Olivia, get a grip.

I turn and take the coat when he shoves it into my hands. "Thank you."

"Let me get a cab for you." When he reaches to open the pub's door, his arm brushes the side of my breast.

We both look down. I almost groan aloud at the sight of my pebbled nipples under my blouse. I should make up an excuse about catching a draft from the doorway, but ignoring the fact that I'm feeling a rush of desire is the route I'm going to take.

I stay silent.

He clears his throat. "Let me help you with that."

"With what?" My voice is high-pitched. I raise my coat until it's covering my blouse.

"This." He tugs the coat from my grasp and holds it out, waiting for me to slip into it.

I tie the belt before I look up and into his face. He's studying me carefully. I run my finger along my bottom lip, hoping that a piece of food isn't lingering there.

His eyes follow the path of my finger.

I drop my hand immediately and glance out the door. "I'll get that cab now."

"Allow me," he says in that sexy baritone voice.

I don't argue because there's no point. He's already holding the door open, waiting for me to walk through.

I do.

The cool evening air hits me. I tug the collar of my coat up to ward off the chill from the light wind.

He approaches the street, taking one large step off the curb.

That act alone earns him bravery points in my book. Only a born and raised New Yorker would risk life and limb to get that close to the approaching traffic.

His gaze darts from the cars stopped at the light down the street to where I'm standing a few feet away, safely on the sidewalk.

"You're headed uptown?" he calls to me.

I nod and jerk a thumb in that direction.

He opens his mouth as if he's about to ask another question but his attention is pulled back to the traffic as the light turns green and an onslaught of vehicles approach.

He takes another measured step toward the traffic, his arm flying into the air.

A taxi slows as it approaches. Alexander turns to me with a broad smile on his face. "Your chariot awaits."

I can't hold back a small grin as I move toward him. He's already opened the back door of the car for me.

I stop before I slide in. "Thank you again."

"It's my pleasure. When you're not in a rush, you'll share a drink with me."

"Maybe." My gaze stays locked on his face.

"You will." He flashes me a cocky grin.

I want to wipe that arrogant smirk off his mouth...with my lips.

"You in or out?" A thick Brooklyn accent asks.

I pop my head into the cab. "I'm in."

"Where are we headed?" The driver asks.

"Broadway and Eighty-first," I reply instantly.

"Get home safely, Olivia." Alexander takes a step back as I move to get into the car.

I look into his blue eyes. They're the color of the ocean or the sky on a clear summer day. They're as beautiful as the rest of him.

I chase away my sudden infatuation with his eyes with a heavy intake of breath. "You too, Alexander."

Once I'm in the cab, he closes the door and taps the roof.

The driver effortlessly steers the car into the traffic as I resist the urge to turn back to see if Alexander is watching me drive away.

CHAPTER FIFTEEN

OLIVIA

"YOU SCARED the hell out of me, Kate," I say tightly, trying to keep my voice from cracking.

I reach to pick up my keys from the floor. They landed there after Kate opened her apartment door just as I was sliding the key into the lock of mine.

Screaming my name in excitement, she grabbed my shoulders from behind.

That sent both of my hands into the air, and my keys and phone crashing to the floor.

My phone was my first concern, but luckily the heavy-duty case that I was talked into buying by the smartphone salesman saved my screen.

"What are you doing here?" I unlock my door and take a step into my place. "I thought you were going to your store."

Following me inside, she flicks on the light switch. "I have a confession to make."

Watching her lock the door, I shrug out of my trench coat. "What confession?"

She takes the coat from me and hangs it on the rack near the doorway. "I'm sorry for scaring you, Liv. You look like you might pass out. Do you want to sit down?"

"I'm fine." I manage a small smile. "Tell me about the confession."

She leads the way into my living room. She's changed since I saw her at the restaurant. She's now dressed in navy blue yoga shorts and a white T-shirt.

I'm envious. I want to trade my skirt and blouse for pajamas, but we still have plans to try on dresses to wear to the symphony.

She takes her usual spot on my couch, patting the spot next to her. "Sit."

I do, kicking off my shoes in the process.

I breathe an audible sigh of relief. "My feet are killing me."

A small giggle escapes her. "I know the feeling. I couldn't get my heels off fast enough tonight."

I look down at her feet and the thick gray wool socks covering them. "Did you go back to your store after dinner?"

"That's the confession. I didn't." She catches my gaze. "I thought you'd appreciate some alone time with Alexander, so I lied about that."

I can't be mad at her. I've done the same to her, but Kate's heart is still caught back in a relationship that ended years ago. She dates but those men never measure up to her ex-fiancé. He bailed on her just before their wedding.

"I didn't overstep, did I?" She blinks innocently. "You can't blame me, Liv. It's obvious that he's interested in you."

"He's not," I whisper.

She heaves a sigh. "He's interested in you."

"He makes me nervous," I laugh. "I don't feel like myself when I'm around him."

Her brow furrows. "What do you mean?"

I scan her face. I only see concern there. Kate wants me to be happy. I want the same for her. She's heard enough of my tales about the men I've slept with to know that I don't rush into anything, not even first dates.

I can be honest with her. She'll never judge me.

"I feel flustered whenever I see him." I rub the back of my neck. "I know his type. I avoid his type so I don't understand why I'm feeling…"

"Attracted to him," she interrupts me.

I shrug. "Is that what I'm feeling?"

"What's his type?" she asks without answering my rhetorical question. "Define what type of man Alexander Donato is."

I pause to think about it. "First impressions are everything and that day he came into the boutique I saw an arrogant, self-absorbed jerk who wanted everyone in his vicinity to bow to his demands."

She shakes her head. "You saw a man desperate to give his nephew a birthday gift to remember."

"You weren't there," I point out with a laugh. "You didn't see what he was like that day."

The corner of her mouth lifts into a lopsided grin. "I was there tonight. I saw what he was like."

I raise a brow to question what that means.

"He was polite and considerate. He's charming," she says quietly. "He couldn't take his eyes off of you, Olivia."

"He wanted to buy me a drink after you and Jack left." I pinch the bridge of my nose. "I made a fool of myself. My phone was dead. I thought he was trying to help me with my nipples, and…"

"What?" She laughs aloud. "You have to explain that one. You thought he was trying to help you with your nipples?"

I laugh too because I know how it must sound to her. "That came out wrong."

"You think?" She wraps an arm around my shoulder. "I'm sure if he could he'd help with your nipples and all the other bits of you."

I cover my face with my hands. "Let's not go there."

"Why not?" She squeezes my shoulder. "You're attracted to each other. Why not act on it?"

"Well…" I start to protest, but can't think of any reason why I shouldn't consider having sex with Alexander.

"Don't overthink it." She moves to stand. "Just go with what you're feeling in the moment. Sometimes it's good to be spontaneous."

She gave me the same advice last week when I couldn't decide what to order for dinner.

"It's time to try on some dresses." She reaches for my hand. "Let's find you something to wear to the symphony that will blow Alexander's mind so later that night you can blow him."

I let her tug me to my feet. "I don't blow on the first date."

"You're no fun." She grins and squeezes my hand. "Never change, Liv. You're a fiercely independent woman that any man would be lucky to spend time with."

"I hate that he makes me nervous." I bow my head. "It makes me feel out of control."

Her fingers find my chin and she tips it up until our eyes meet. "Nervous can be good. He's different than other men you've met. That's not necessarily a bad thing."

I nod. "You're right."

"Take it one step at a time." She grins and starts walking toward my bedroom. "Step one is wardrobe selection. Let's get to it."

CHAPTER SIXTEEN

ALEXANDER

I'LL NEVER tire of the high I feel after a performance like that.

It was exhilarating and as the crowd rose to their feet and cheered, I reveled in their adoration for the orchestra.

My job is to sculpt the music into a piece of art that every person on the stage can be proud of. I may guide them, but they are the true masters of the journey.

I take another deep breath as I gaze around the room.

I notice Olivia before she notices me.

She's already arrived at the private cocktail reception that's being held in the lobby. Dressed in a backless black dress and black heels, she's flawless. Her long dark hair is styled into a knot at the base of her neck.

She looks elegant, almost regal. It's no wonder that men are turning in her direction once they catch sight of her.

I slip the bowtie from around my neck and tuck it into the pocket of my tuxedo jacket. I unbutton my collar for comfort.

Pushing my hair back from my forehead, I approach Olivia. She's having an animated conversation with Kate, Jack, and the female client he brought with him.

He's banking on the fact that she'll work with him to invest more of the fortune she inherited from her late husband.

"I bet you didn't think you'd ever see me again, Al."

The sound of a female voice lures my attention to the left.

Al.

It's the name I sometimes toss out when I meet a woman I envision spending one night with. Back in college, I'd pull a fake name out of thin air, but the effort isn't worth it anymore.

Al is impersonal enough that it doesn't impact me when a woman screams it during an orgasm.

I take in the woman next to me. She's blonde-haired, brown-eyed and wearing a tight red dress.

All signs point to her being a former lover of mine, yet I can't place her.

That should embarrass me, but it doesn't. I have fun. I'm careful and respectful enough to make it clear to the women I sleep with that my true passion is music and I'm not looking for anything serious.

"That was an incredible performance tonight." She moves a step closer to me, her perfume floating in the air between us.

The scent is familiar.

"Thank you," I reply out of habit.

Whenever I was handed a compliment when I first started conducting, I'd push for more. I'd want to know what the person I was talking to felt during the performance. I'd question them about the nuances in the music and how they interpreted them.

It wasn't until I realized that most of them had no idea what I was talking about that I switched to a simple '*thank you*' as a response.

I glance over at Olivia. She's turned her attention to a man in a navy blue suit. I can only see his profile, but it's clear that he's checking her out from head-to-toe.

"If you'll excuse me," I say gently to the woman next to me.

I won't fumble for a name I can't remember. I won't offer any hollow remarks about how great it is to see her again.

I don't remember her. Pointing that out will only humiliate her.

"Why are you rushing away?" Her hand grabs hold of my forearm. "We should talk."

I look down at her hand and the perfectly manicured black fingernails that are digging into the sleeve of my jacket. Just as I'm reaching to pry her hand free, I catch sight of the tattoo on her wrist.

It's an arrow.

A flash of memories assaults me as I slide my gaze back up to her face.

Those eyes, the thin lips and that body.

I might have thought she was remarkable at the time, but now I see why I've forgotten her so quickly.

She's attractive which is why I picked her up and took her home that night, but there's nothing about her that stuck with me and implanted itself into my memory.

I grab her hand in mine and twist it from my arm. "What the fuck are you doing here?"

Her body trembles under my touch but not in the way it did when I was between her legs. This is different. Fear punctuates her movements now.

"Al." Her voice is barely more than a whisper. "What's gotten into you?"

"You're a thief," I seethe. "You fucking stole from me."

"What?" She blinks. "What are you talking about?"

This woman won't win any awards for her lackluster acting abilities. Her pulse has increased. Her breathing is labored. Small beads of sweat are pooling above her red stained lips.

"Where the hell is the jersey you took from my apartment?"

She flashes a smile that I suspect is meant to disarm me. It doesn't. "I have no idea what you mean."

"You left my apartment while I was asleep and you took an autographed Trey Hale jersey."

"Me?" She tugs her hand to free it from my grasp, but I'm not letting go. "The only thing I took home with me that night is the memory of how good your big cock felt inside of me."

"Jesus. Lower your voice." I glance over my shoulder at the people passing us.

I don't need anyone to hear this shit.

"What's your name?" I lean down until I'm face-to-face with her. "Tell me your name."

"You don't remember my name?" She yanks her hand free. "You're an asshole."

"You're a thief," I counter as I give the lapels of my jacket a tug to straighten it. "I should call the police."

Her hand disappears into her clutch purse to retrieve a tube of lip gloss. "What would you say to them? You have no proof that I took anything that belonged to you."

"You took it." I exhale harshly. "What did you do with it?"

"What did you do with my panties?" She applies the lip gloss before tossing it back into her purse. "I forgot a brand new pair of panties at your place. Can I stop by and pick them up or are you keeping them as a souvenir to remember me by?"

"I threw them in the trash." I hold back a smile. "The only thing memorable about you is your penchant for taking things that don't belong to you."

"Fine." She glares at me. "If you take me home with you tonight I'll show you just how memorable I can be. In exchange, I'll give you back the jersey."

I study her face. I don't know what I saw in her that night. She's cute, but there's nothing remotely unique about her.

I lean in closer to her, lowering my voice. "You're proposing that if I fuck you again, you'll give me the jersey back?"

She nods. "Anyway you look at it, you win. You get me and your jersey."

Shaking my head, I work to control the urge to laugh in her face. "I've had my fill of you. Keep the jersey. I'm not interested."

The corners of her lips dip into a frown. "What?"

"I'm not interested," I repeat in a low tone.

"I bought a ticket for this just to see you." She rubs her forehead. "It was expensive. So was this dress and these shoes weren't cheap. I even bought a new pair of panties just for you."

"Your loss." I brush past her. "If you'll excuse me, there's someone I need to talk to."

I take a step toward where Olivia was, but she's gone.

I look around the room and curse under my breath when I don't spot her anywhere. That one-night stand I just finished talking to might have cost me more than an autographed jersey. She may have stolen my chance to talk to the woman I can't stop thinking about.

CHAPTER SEVENTEEN

OLIVIA

"I'M TELLING YOU, Liv, I don't think she's his date." Studying herself in the mirror, Kate brushes a strand of hair from the side of her face. "He looked pissed off."

I did catch the expression on Alexander's face before we left the lobby to use the restroom. He wasn't smiling at the blonde who he was holding onto. His eyes were intense and his lips were set in a firm line.

He didn't notice Kate and I as we breezed past him on our way here.

"It doesn't matter." I shrug off her comments. "We can leave. Do you want to head to a club?"

Her gaze drops to the black lace dress she's wearing. "I'm not ready to bail yet. We put on our Sunday best for this thing. I say we head back out there, drink another glass of champagne and mingle."

It's the last thing I want to do.

I had a long day at work. I intended to leave early so I'd have extra time to prepare for tonight, but a last minute emergency at the boutique on Fifth Avenue kept me there until almost six o'clock which meant I had to rush home, shower and get myself together so we could be here by seven.

It's not uncommon for there to be an issue on a Friday afternoon but this one was catastrophic. The inventory for our one-day-only sale tomorrow hadn't shown up by three p.m.

I spent the next two-and-a-half hours on the phone tracking it down. It'll be delivered just after midnight. That means Steph and her employees have to pull an all-nighter to get everything set up before the store opens at nine a.m. sharp.

There's a gnawing pang of guilt inside of me that keeps telling me to get my ass down there to help.

Any other night I would have, but I wanted to be here tonight. I was excited to watch Alexander lead the orchestra and he did it with graceful precision.

I was in awe as I watched the movement of his hands, his arms and his entire body as the musicians kept their eyes pinned to him.

I could feel the music enveloping me, flowing through me. Kate was just as captivated as I was. Even my cousin, Trey, was mesmerized by the performance, as were Buck and his ex-wife.

"Stop thinking about Alexander and that woman." Kate playfully pinches my bicep. "He's bound to attract a lot of attention tonight."

I know that she's right. This is his opening night. The sheer volume of the applause when he was introduced was deafening.

I'd never heard of Alexander Donato before he walked

into the boutique, but apparently, a lot of people know exactly who he is.

"Let's go find Trey," I suggest as I adjust the front of my dress. "I haven't had a chance to talk to him tonight."

"As long as I have a glass of champagne in my hand, I'll talk to whoever you want me to."

I link arms with her as we start toward the door.

I may never experience another evening like this, so I need to embrace every minute of it, even if I don't see Alexander before the night is over.

———

I SPOT Trey as soon as we exit the washroom. He's standing next to a blonde haired woman in a black dress. She has a breathtaking strand of pearls around her neck.

My cousin may have arrived alone to the performance, but something tells me he won't be leaving by himself.

"Livi, come here," Trey calls out, motioning me over. "There's someone you need to meet."

I glance across the lobby to where Alexander was standing with the woman in the red dress, but he's not there anymore.

Maybe what I mistook for anger was a prelude to passion and they've already left.

"You visit with Trey," Kate says as she motions toward the right. "I'm going to hunt down another glass of champagne."

"I'll catch up with you in a few minutes?"

Her eyes search my face. "Take your time and enjoy yourself. Find me when you can."

I nod and continue making my way toward Trey and the blonde woman, weaving around people as they move past me.

"This is my cousin Olivia." The words are out of Trey's mouth before I'm in front of him. "Olivia, this is Phoebe Costa."

I take the woman's left hand in mine when she offers it. My eyes hone in on the simple gold band on her ring finger.

Trey has always been protective of me, but that works both ways. I subtly point out what I just noticed. "It's nice to meet you, Mrs. Costa."

Her smile is bright and bold. "My students call me that. It's Phoebe."

"You're a teacher?" I drop her hand and return the smile. "What do you teach?"

"Third grade." She sighs. "I love it."

I thought about teaching when I was in high school, but business lured me in. I've never looked back.

"I'm so happy that I have a chance to thank you." She glances over at Trey. "My husband and I still can't believe what you two did for our son."

My gaze slides to my cousin. I furrow my brow because I feel lost.

Trey comes to my rescue immediately. "Phoebe is Alvin's mom. She's Alexander's sister."

The pieces of the puzzle fall together instantly. This woman is the mother of Alexander's nephew.

"Alvin," I say her son's name quietly. "I'm so happy that everything worked out for him. Trey is the one to thank. He's the one who stepped up to bat and saved the day."

They laugh in unison at my lame attempt at a baseball joke.

"What have we here?" Alexander's raspy voice weakens my knees as he approaches from behind me.

I look over my shoulder and lock eyes with him. He gives me a wicked smile.

"You were brilliant up there tonight, Alex." Phoebe's words draw my attention back to her. I see pride beaming in her eyes as she looks at her brother.

"You were," Trey chimes in. "I admit I wasn't a fan of the symphony before tonight, but I'm impressed."

"Thanks, Trey," Alexander says as he steps into place next to me. "I'll never win a World Series, but I get the job done."

Phoebe's smile widens. "I've had a blast, but I need to get home. My mother-in-law is watching Alvin tonight and I'd like to spend time with both of them before he goes to sleep."

"The driver who brought you is waiting to take you home." Alexander types something into the phone he just pulled from his jacket pocket. "He'll be waiting for you right where he dropped you off."

Phoebe takes a step forward to embrace her brother. "Tonight was magical, Alex. Thank you for everything."

He kisses her square in the middle of the forehead. "It wouldn't have been complete without you here."

"I wouldn't have missed this for anything," she whispers back. "Call me tomorrow."

"I'll walk you to your car," Trey offers as Phoebe takes a step back. "I'm going to hit a bar in Times Square for a few beers with some teammates."

I watch them head out, acutely aware of how close Alexander's body is to mine.

His hand finds the small of my back sending a rush of goose bumps over my skin. "You look beautiful tonight, Olivia."

I look up and into his eyes. "Thank you."

His gaze slowly travels over my face. "Are you enjoying yourself?"

I swallow past the lump in my throat. "I am. It's been a night to remember."

He leans in until I can feel his lips brush against my ear. "It's been the start of a night to remember. The best is yet to come."

CHAPTER EIGHTEEN

OLIVIA

THERE'S a promise laced into his words, but there's hesitation in his eyes and his touch.

His hand is still resting on the small of my back, but his gaze is searching mine for something. There's a question there that he wants to ask me. I sense it.

"Alexander!" A man's voice startles us both enough that we pull apart.

Alexander rakes his hand through his hair, causing the strands to take their own liberties. He doesn't look as put together as he did on stage. He's imperfect now, in the most enticing way.

"This is only going to take a minute, Olivia." He looks over at two older men in black suits approaching us. One is waving frantically, while the other follows closely on his heel. "That's my music teacher from grade school and his husband. I invited them tonight. I need to spend a few minutes with them."

I smile. "He must be so proud of you."

"He taught me a lot." He moves his hand to touch my forearm. "He taught me to respect music, to honor its unique voice. I wouldn't be where I am today without him."

I inch back when the two men reach us. The one who was waving frantically takes Alexander's hand, patting him on the bicep. "Would you look at you? I always knew this was your destiny."

"All thanks to you, Chris." Alexander smiles at him before he turns to the other man. "It's good to see, Wayne."

"You too, Alexander."

I start to inch backward on my heels, realizing that this is a private moment that I shouldn't be witnessing.

"This is Olivia Hull." Alexander shoots me a smile. "Olivia, this is Wayne Rollington and my hero, Chris Morgenson."

I shake both men's hands, wondering if they've jumped to the incorrect conclusion that I'm more to Alexander than an acquaintance.

"I got your text message earlier." Chris shoves both hands into the pockets of his pants. "I have to say that I didn't know if you'd want to help us out, Alexander, but I'm grateful."

"Me too," Wayne adds. "We didn't know what to do until you came along."

"It's not a problem," Alexander says brusquely. "We'll work out the details via text."

Chris nods as if he's reading between the lines. "That'll work."

I bow my head. Whatever they are discussing is private. It's not meant for my ears.

These men don't know me, so I'm not surprised that Alexander feels the need to keep the conversation limited to the three of them.

"We won't keep you two." Chris squeezes Alexander's shoulder. "You've done well for yourself, Alexander."

"You had a hand in that."

Chris laughs. "I taught you the basics. You took that knowledge and ran with it."

"We'll be in touch." Wayne extends his hand to Alexander and then me. "It was good to meet you, Olivia."

"You too," I say softly as they walk away.

Once they're out of sight, Alexander's hand is back on the small of my back.

His touch ignites something within me. I know he can feel it.

"I don't want another interruption." His voice is low and rough. "Let's get out of here."

I suck in a trembling breath. "You want to leave?"

"I need to leave," he corrects me. "I want to be alone with you."

He's not outright suggesting that we go back to his place, but the implication is there. I'm not ready for that.

"There's a wine bar a few blocks from here. It's quiet." I take my fate into my own hands. We can share a drink, maybe a first kiss, but getting naked with this man tonight isn't going to happen.

My body wants it, but it's too soon. Regret will crawl into bed with me the moment he rolls out of it.

His jaw flexes. "Lead the way, Olivia."

———

"YOU WERE serious when you said this place is quiet." Alexander shrugs out of his jacket and hangs it over the back of a chair. "How in the hell is a place like this not packed on a Friday night?"

It's a good question that I don't have an answer to.

Kate and I stumbled on this wine bar months ago after we exited a movie theater. We stopped in to have a glass of chardonnay, and it's now become one of our favorite haunts in this part of the city.

It's quaint, quiet and the selection of wine is extensive.

A few of the stools next to the massive bar are occupied, and two of the square wooden tables are surrounded by groups of people, but this corner where we situated ourselves is unoccupied if you don't count the couple who are staring into each other's eyes, oblivious to everyone around them.

I took a seat at a table diagonal from where they are. Alexander didn't say a word as he held the back of my chair when I sat down. He was considerate enough to help me with my trench coat as I slipped it off my shoulders. After carefully folding it in two, he laid it over the back of the same chair where he just placed his tuxedo jacket.

Alexander's mouth quirks when he sees a server approaching our table. "You'll order for us both, Olivia."

I don't hesitate in telling the server what I'm in the mood for. I listen to her recommendations. Not one of them fits the bill of what my palate is craving.

I can feel Alexander's eyes on me when I finally suggest two glasses of a dark red that Kate and I sampled a few weeks ago.

"You know your wine," he says when the server walks away. "I'm impressed."

"That I drink a lot of wine?" I lean back in the chair.

He shakes his head and glances down at where I've placed my hands on the edge of the table. "I have a question."

"Ask away."

His eyes narrow. "Are you involved with anyone?"

The question catches me off-guard although it shouldn't.

He doesn't know my relationship status. He's never asked and I don't think Trey would be quick to offer up a detail about me that's so personal.

"If I've overstepped," he continues, his lips inching up into a smile. "You'll forgive me."

He's so confident. I'd find that annoying if he weren't sexy-as-sin.

"I'm not involved," I say directly. "Are you?"

He holds my gaze before he answers. "No."

I'm tempted to ask him about the woman in the red dress that I saw him with at the cocktail reception, but I won't. That was a private moment between him and someone else.

"You'll come home with me tonight, Olivia."

My brows pop as I replay the words in my mind. There wasn't a question mark at the end of that sentence. He's assuming that I'm going home with him.

He looks calm and controlled as he stares at me across the table.

"No. I won't, Alexander."

His jaw clenches. "Have I misread the energy between us?"

I suppose it's a better response than *why*, although it's just logistics. He wants an explanation for why I'm not willing to jump into his bed tonight.

I look up as the server places a glass of wine on a cocktail napkin in front of me before she does the same for Alexander.

She waits patiently for me to sample it, but I know if I pick it up now, I'll down the fragrant red liquid in one gulp.

"It's fine." I smile at her. "Thank you."

She glances at Alexander before she nods silently and leaves.

He takes a healthy sip of the wine, his eyes locked on mine the entire time.

"Olivia," he begins as he lowers the glass. "I want..."

"I don't sleep with men I don't know." I gloss my tongue over my bottom lip. "We just met."

He inhales deeply, his gaze dropping to the wine glass in front of me before he looks into my eyes again. "Have dinner with me tomorrow night."

It's not the reaction I anticipated. I thought we'd finish our drinks, part ways and that would be the end of my story with Alexander Donato.

"Don't look so surprised, Olivia." He leans in closer to me. "You'll get to know me better and then we'll revisit this discussion."

"This discussion?" I parrot back.

"My intense desire to fuck you isn't going anywhere." He moves so his lips are almost touching mine. "We'll have dinner tomorrow and take it from there."

I pull back so I can find some air to breathe that doesn't taste like him. "I won't sleep with you tomorrow either."

The corner of his mouth twitches into an almost smile. "Duly noted. I'll pick you up at eight o'clock tomorrow evening."

"You don't know where I live," I point out, feeling a blush taking over my cheeks.

"You live somewhere in the vicinity of Broadway and Eighty-first."

"How do you know that?"

He takes another sip of the wine before he answers me. "I overheard you telling it to the cab driver outside the pub."

He remembered?

"You can tell me your address or I can ring the buzzer of every apartment in every building on that block until I find you." He drops his voice. "Your choice."

I can't help but smile. "I'll tell you my address."

He slides his fingers across the screen of his phone. "And your phone number."

I give both without hesitation, watching as he enters my information into his smartphone.

Once the phone is back on the table, he lifts his wine glass in the air. "Let's toast to getting to know each other better."

I lift my glass and clink it against his.

The wolfish grin on his face is telling me that tomorrow night will be just as interesting as tonight has been.

I can't wait.

CHAPTER NINETEEN

ALEXANDER

OLIVIA LIVES CLOSER to Amsterdam than Broadway. I'm not surprised she gave the taxi driver the address of an intersection a block from where she lives.

Most New Yorkers would rather walk the few extra steps than pay the added fare for the driver to circle the block to get onto a one-way street.

"Where are we going for dinner?" She looks up at me expectantly.

I haven't seen her dressed like this before, which is why I requested it via text earlier today.

I reached out this afternoon to confirm that we were still on for eight o'clock. I anticipated she'd ask what to wear.

When she did, I told her we were keeping it casual tonight.

The faded jeans and white sweater she's wearing are perfect.

Her hair is down around her shoulders.

She looks relaxed and content. I'm hoping to keep her that way for the duration of the evening.

"We're having pizza." I reach for her hand. "We can walk there from here."

Her eyes rake me from head-to-toe taking in the jeans, gray V-neck sweater and dark blue blazer I'm wearing.

"Pizza?" Her button nose scrunches.

I cross my arms over my chest. "You're not a fan?"

She taps the toe of her black boot against the floor.

We're still in the lobby of her building. I buzzed her when I arrived, hoping for an invitation up to her apartment, but she answered with a curt, "I'll be down in five."

It was more like fifteen, but I busied myself with returning text messages from Phoebe and Jack.

When she finally stepped off the elevator, any frustration I felt vanished at the sight of her.

"It's never my first choice," she admits. "Besides, I've lived in this neighborhood for months and I know for a fact that there isn't a decent pizza place within walking distance of here."

Honesty. It's refreshing.

"Five hundred and fifty-two people on Yelp would disagree with that. They all gave the place a five-star review."

"I'm not one of them."

I laugh aloud. "Apparently not. What do you want to eat, Olivia?"

"I've had a craving all week."

"For?" I arch a brow.

I don't give a fuck what it is because I know she's not craving me, yet. I'll take her to any restaurant in the city if it means I'm a step closer to feeling her body against mine.

"A lobster roll," she says quietly. "There's this restaurant in the Financial District. They make lobster rolls just like the ones I have in Boston when I go there, and because it matters to you, their Yelp score is…"

She scrolls a finger over her phone's screen. "Give me a minute to find it, but I guarantee they're rated higher than the pizza place you wanted to go to."

I watch her fingers tap over the screen, moving with deliberate precision.

"Here it is," she announces with a smile. "Their rating is…"

"Inconsequential," I interrupt. "Put your phone away, Olivia. If you have a craving, I'll satisfy it."

A blush creeps over her cheeks. "I just want a lobster roll, Alexander."

"It's a start." I hold out my hand. "This is step one in getting to know each other better."

"Step one," she repeats as she takes my hand.

———

"SINCE YOU ATE two lobster rolls, I take it you approve of my choice for dinner." She smiles widely.

I nod as I finish off the last of the beer in my glass. We've been here for over an hour. The service was quick; too quick. My desire to learn more about Olivia was put on hold because of the complimentary breadsticks and the entrees, which arrived before our drinks.

She's nervous. I can tell. Her leg has been vibrating since we sat in this booth.

I wanted to slide in next to her, but she teetered so close to the edge that I had no choice but to take a seat on the bench across from her.

"How long have you worked at Liore?" I ask before she has a chance to call it a night. I'm anticipating that happening at any moment since her gaze keeps diving to the antique silver men's watch on her wrist.

My questions about that will have to wait for another time. I'm hoping it's not a treasured memento of a long lost lover. I don't handle competition with ease, even if it's only grounded in memories.

When I'm with a woman, I want her undivided attention. I give her as much, so I expect the same, whether that's for a night, a week or in one case, two years.

"Forever," she answers effortlessly. "I started as a sales associate at the store on Fifth Avenue years ago."

"You've always worked for the company?"

She shifts in her seat. "Foster Enterprises is an amazing organization. They treat all of their employees with respect. I'm honored that I'm part of their team."

It's a canned response that would bring a wide grin to the face of her boss, Gabriel Foster. I've spent time with the man recently.

His family is his priority, but his company is a close second. He'd take pride in hearing those words coming from one of his employees.

"What about you?" She takes the lead and asks a question of her own. "What made you want to be a conductor?"

"Music," I go on, "I've always loved classical music. I studied the cello and piano when I was a kid. Went to college and earned a degree. From there I traveled, played, learned more, and when someone I admired suggested I consider conducting, I gave it a shot."

The details of where, when and who don't matter. A broad view of how I ended up on that stage last night is all she's looking for.

Studying my face, she brushes a strand of hair back

behind her ear. Her lips purse before she speaks. "Do you believe everyone can learn how to play an instrument?"

"Yes," I answer without reservation. "The ability to play is about technique."

Resting her elbow on the table, she leans toward me. "I have to disagree."

She's failed miserably at learning how to play an instrument. It's a story I've heard far too often in my life from people who couldn't master the piano, a guitar or a violin.

"Did your piano teacher quit during your first lesson?"

Her brows shoot up and a giggle escapes her. "Third lesson."

"How old were you?" I lean forward as well until my hands are almost touching hers on the tabletop.

"Seven."

"You tried again?" I hold back the urge to smile.

"Never," she answers on a sigh.

I glide the tip of my index finger over her thumb. "Why not?"

She gazes down at the movement of my hand. "I hate failing."

Perhaps we have more in common than I thought.

I trail my finger from the base of her thumb to her wrist, circling a tight path over her soft skin. "I'll teach you."

"You like a challenge," she whispers.

I grab her wrist in my hand. Turning it over, I bring it to my lips. I kiss the tender skin. "I love a challenge."

Her eyes lock on mine. "I'll remember that."

"Good." I kiss her skin one last time before I let her wrist slip from my grasp. "That's one thing you've learned about me. You know me better than you did yesterday."

Her beautiful lips curve into a soft smile. "True, but not well enough to revisit our discussion from last night."

"Understood." I motion for the server. "I'll settle up and we can head out."

"Where to?" Her voice is soft.

"Your choice." I tug my wallet from my suit pocket. "You chose this place. Our next move is in your hands."

CHAPTER TWENTY

OLIVIA

I TOOK IT AS A CHALLENGE. When Alexander told me that I could choose where we'd spend time after dinner, I almost bailed on him.

I'm still nervous whenever I'm around him.

My pulse ticked up to a feverish pace when he wrapped his long fingers around my wrist.

The whisper of his full lips against my skin brought up an unexpected moan that I had to bite back.

I want more time with him, so I brought him here.

I study his profile as he takes in the sign hanging over the door of this non-descript building two blocks from Times Square.

"The Pink Parlor," he reads the sign slowly.

"That's right." I nod.

"What happens inside the Pink Parlor, Olivia?" he asks as a couple breezes past us, walking down the sidewalk arm-in-arm.

I watch until they round the corner. "Use your imagination."

His brow perks. "That's dangerous."

I laugh. "You're a music lover. The Pink Parlor is famous for music. I think it's a good fit."

He glances at the building again. Dark blinds cover the windows, and the glass door is peppered with flyers from businesses that inhabit this block.

"I trust you." He reaches for the handle on the door.

As soon as he opens it, pop music greets us both.

A smile ghosts his mouth. "I can't wait to see what's inside."

I can't wait to see if he'll command the stage the way he did last night.

———

I SHOULDN'T HAVE DOUBTED Alexander's ability to captivate any audience.

The people here tonight are an eclectic mix of young and old. I can't tell if anyone recognizes him, but they all love what he's doing on the stage.

Women are whistling, men are pumping their fists in the air and almost every person in the Pink Parlor is on their feet, dancing right along with Alexander.

I've never brought a date to this karaoke bar.

I've come here with Kate a handful of times, and once with her and her friend, Tilly.

Tonight is a brand new experience for me.

"Your boyfriend is awesome." A middle-aged woman elbows me in the side. "He's the life of the party."

I laugh. "He's not my boyfriend."

"He's available?" She stares at the circular stage. "Do you

happen to know if he's into fifty-something divorced women?"

I wiggle both brows. "You can ask him as soon as the song is over."

She shakes a finger at me. "No way. I'm going to lead the charge for an encore as soon as this song is done."

I glance back at the stage to catch Alexander looking right at me as the song drifts into another chorus.

The crowd joins in, singing right along with him.

I shouldn't be surprised. When he took the stage and asked for requests, it was a man who yelled out, "Never Gonna Give You Up."

Alexander called back that he knew all the lyrics before the band started playing.

He can sing. He can dance too.

I'm starting to wonder if there's anything Alexander Donato can't do well.

As the song ends, the crowd starts chanting for an encore. Alexander's hand pops into the air as he brings the microphone back to his lips. "I need a break, folks. Thanks for making me feel like a rock star for one night."

Laughter fills the room as he steps down from the stage taking the stairs two at a time.

The people gathered near the stage part to let him pass through. Some of them pat him on the back. Others shake his hand.

By the time he reaches me, I'm grinning from ear-to-ear.

He picks up the bottle of beer he ordered before he hit the stage. "It's your turn, Olivia."

"Not tonight." I shake my head. "My throat is a little scratchy."

"Is that so?" He leans forward, his finger hovering over the skin of my neck. "You didn't mention that earlier."

I pretend to cough. "It just started."

"Take the stage." He motions toward it with his beer. "We had an agreement."

"Did we?" I feign surprise even though he's right.

I dared him to sing in front of strangers because I thought he'd refuse to do it. I was wrong. I was so wrong.

"We did," he affirms. "I kept my end of the bargain. It's time for you to keep yours."

I can't follow him.

Dozens of people were spellbound by the show he put on. I'll barely turn a head once I start singing.

The band begins to play as a woman grabs the microphone and starts crooning an Adele ballad off key.

That I can follow.

"I'll go next," I promise as I take the last sip of my glass of house red wine.

"Let me guess." He rests his hand on the table, leaning against it. "You're inspired by her so you'll be serenading us with your version of an Adele song."

I cross my arms over my chest. "That's not my style."

He places his beer bottle on the tabletop. "What's your style?"

"Britney."

His eyes narrow. "Spears?"

I look over at the stage and the woman who is now on her knees pouring her heart into the song as the crowd sways back and forth listening to her every word.

When I turn back to Alexander, his eyes are pinned to my face.

"I know the lyrics to all of her songs," I say proudly.

"I can't wait to see this." He pushes the sleeves of his sweater up to reveal his muscular forearms. "I'll be cheering you on."

I take a swallow from his beer, turn on my heel and march toward the stage, hoping with everything I am that I pull this off.

CHAPTER TWENTY-ONE

ALEXANDER

I CAN'T REMEMBER the last time I had this much fun.

Olivia can sing. She belted out her own rendition of "Baby One More Time" as the crowd cheered her on.

Any reservations she had when the song started were gone by the end of the first chorus.

She was beaming as she pranced around the stage, shaking her lush ass.

I was hard halfway through the song and aching to be inside of her by the time she rushed back to our table.

I had to sit to hide my erection.

We're outside now, standing in front of the Pink Parlor while she contemplates our next move.

I was sure she'd want to head home, but she's game for the night to continue. So am I.

Every moment we spend together brings me closer to fucking her.

Jesus, I want to fuck this woman.

"You're thinking about dessert, aren't you?" she asks as she looks down the barren sidewalk.

I shake my head. "I'm thinking about your ass."

Her hand flies to her mouth. "I'm not having that discussion tonight, Alexander."

I shove my hands into the front pocket of my jeans. "You've made that clear, Olivia. I'll make it clear that I think you have an incredible ass. It's merely an observation, not a prelude to a discussion you're not ready to have yet."

She ponders that for a second. "I could go for something sweet. Do you want to get ice cream?"

If I were Alvin's age, I'd be all over the idea of ice cream at midnight, but my tastes lean toward other things at this time of night.

The taste of her cunt and the sound of her cries as she climaxes both top my list of things I want.

It's not my choice though. I've been encouraging her all night to take the lead. I'm not going to shift the balance now. "Ice cream it is."

She darts toward the street. "We need a cab."

I move too, circling one arm around her from behind. I rest my hand on her stomach, leaning in so I can whisper into her ear. "If we walk a block over, we'll have an easier time finding one."

Her body relaxes as her hand finds mine. She holds it in place. "After we have ice cream, I'll need to go home."

"You'll want to go home," I correct her as I run my lips over the shell of her ear. "You'll insist on going home alone."

She nods silently.

"You'll think about me when you get there." I splay my fingers and press her against me. I know she can feel my erection. Hell, I want her to feel how hard I am for her.

"I won't," she says quietly.

"You will." I step closer to her. I'm so close that nothing separates the two of us but our clothing.

Her ass wiggles against me. "Will you think about me?"

I nuzzle closer to her, trailing my lips over the side of her neck. "I'll fall asleep thinking of you. I'll wake up thinking about you."

My cock aches for her. I'll jerk off to thoughts of her before I sleep. I'll have to.

Her head falls back against my shoulder. "Tonight has been…"

"A great first step." I slide my hand up her body, between her breasts until I cup it around the front of her neck.

Tilting it back, I glide my lips over her cheek.

"Alexander." My name is barely more than a whisper on her lips.

A sudden burst of noise pulls her away from me. We both turn to the source. It's a group of people exiting the club behind us. They're singing at the top of their lungs.

"Can we skip the ice cream?" She looks up and into my face. "I think I need to call it a night."

I lean down and press a kiss to her forehead. "I understand. Let's get a cab and I'll take you home."

Just as we're about to cross the street, a taxi rounds the corner.

"I'll grab that one." Her hand flies into the air. "I can make it home from here on my own."

I reach to open the back passenger door once the taxi stops. She slips in before I can say anything. "I'll talk to you soon, Olivia."

"Soon," she repeats back, her gaze meeting mine. "Thank you for tonight, Alexander."

I nod before I turn to the driver. "Broadway and Eighty-first."

"Got it," he calls back as I shut the car's door. It pulls away from the curb, abruptly ending a night I'll never forget.

CHAPTER TWENTY-TWO

Olivia

I HEAR Kate's door open before I can get into my apartment. I curse under my breath. I was hoping she'd be fast asleep by now.

"You're alone," she says, disappointment edging her tone. "Alexander didn't want to come home with you?"

I turn and face her, taking in her freshly washed face and red pajamas. "I didn't want him to come home with me."

"Did you have fun?"

I motion for her to follow me into my apartment. Once we're both inside, I lock the door and turn on the lights.

My keys land next to my purse on my coffee table.

"Do you want anything?" I ask as I walk to the kitchen, kicking off my boots on my way. "I can get you some water or juice."

"I'm good," she calls to me.

I grab a bottle of chilled water from my fridge and press the cold plastic to my neck. I feel flush. I know that it has nothing to do with the fact that the cab driver had the heat turned to high in his car.

He explained that he just moved to Manhattan from Florida and he can't tolerate the cold temperatures.

It's not cold. It was barely chilly tonight, but I withstood the heat blasting into my face as he drove me home.

I crack open the lid of the bottle and take a large swallow.

I want to shower and crawl into bed, but I know that Kate's dying to know what happened between Alexander and me tonight.

I can't explain any of it, especially my reaction on the sidewalk outside the club. I was overcome with a raw need to be with him. The intensity surprised me so much that I got in the first cab I saw and ended the date.

"I took him to the Pink Parlor," I announce as I round the corner that leads to my living room.

"You did what?" She asks, adjusting a blanket my mom knit over her legs.

"I didn't think he'd be willing to sing, but he killed it." I laugh.

She moves to lie on her side, resting her head on the arm of the couch. "Classical music has lyrics?"

I stifle a laugh. "His musical taste reaches beyond that."

"What did he sing?" She yawns.

I do the same, covering my mouth with my hand. "Never Gonna Give You Up."

Surprise dances in her eyes. "You're kidding?"

I fall onto a red chair opposite the couch, tucking my legs beneath me. "I'm serious. It was amazing, Kate. He jumped right into it. He owned that song."

"I would have paid money to see that," she says quietly. "Did you sing?"

"Britney." I shrug.

"Classic." She giggles. "You did me proud."

I take another sip of water as I watch her eyelids flutter shut. "We can pick this up tomorrow, Kate. You should get home and into bed."

"I'm fine." She yawns again, tugging the blanket up to her neck. "Tell me what else you two did."

I look down at my hand, remembering what it felt like to hold Alexander's. "He wanted pizza, but I told him that I was craving lobster rolls, so we went to that place in the Financial District. It was good. I had fun."

She doesn't respond so I glance in her direction.

Her eyes are closed, and a faint snoring sound is escaping from her throat every time she inhales.

She's fast asleep.

I don't have the heart to wake her, so I get up and tuck a pillow under her head, adjust the blanket so it's covering her completely and I turn off the lights.

"Goodnight, Kate," I whisper before I kiss her forehead. "Sweet dreams."

———

"DID you have a hot date this weekend, Olivia?"

What the…?

I look up to see Sheryl standing in the doorway of my office. Considering that it's Monday morning and not quite nine a.m., I'm shocked to see her here.

My assistant almost always extends her weekend until at least eleven on Monday mornings.

Today is an exception.

She's dressed in a navy blue skirt and white blouse.

Great.

We're wearing matching outfits today.

"You should have texted me to tell me what not to wear today, Sheryl." I push back from my desk, stand and twirl in place. "We look like bookends."

"You're thirty years younger than me and your curves are still all in the right places. "She mimics grabbing her breasts near her stomach. "If I weren't wearing an extra supportive Liore bra, I'd be arrested for indecency."

I laugh. "Why are you here so early?"

"Can I sit?" She motions toward the two white chairs across from my desk.

"Please." I take a seat in my chair as she closes the door.

She takes a moment to situate herself, carefully crossing her legs and adjusting her skirt. She slides her eyeglasses down her nose as she peers over them at me.

"Are you moving to London?" She points to the laptop on my desk. "I saw the email that Human Resources sent you on Friday afternoon."

I saw it too right before I left the office.

It was the invitation to submit my interest in the position in London. I read through it quickly and then dashed out to help at the store on Fifth Avenue.

I plan to take some time this afternoon to read it over again.

"I'll submit my application, but I have no idea if I'll get the position," I answer honestly. "I hope I do."

"I read the fine print and it says that when it comes to hiring an assistant, you make the call." She jerks a thumb toward herself. "I know someone who works well with you and would love the opportunity to work in the London office."

"You'd move to London to be my assistant?" I'm surprised. I'm actually shocked that she'd consider a life-changing move across the globe.

Sheryl is single. Her divorce was finalized years before we met. Her son and his wife live in Montana with their two young kids. Her daughter is studying at a college in Georgia.

I assumed that she had roots in New York City that would keep her here until she retired.

"I'm due for something new," she tells me. "I've always imagined living in London or Paris. If I don't do it soon, that ship will sail away without me."

I nod, processing everything she just said. "If I get the job in London, I'd want you there beside me, but I might not get it. A lot of people are applying for it."

"You'd be surprised by how few people were invited to apply for it, Olivia." She tosses me a wink. "I have a friend in HR. We met for coffee yesterday and she let a few things slip about the London job."

I resist the urge to question her more because I don't want to compromise my chances. The less I know about what she talked about with her HR friend, the better. "I'll keep my fingers crossed that I land the job."

"Me too." She crosses her index finger over the middle one. "Back to my original question."

"Which was?" I grin.

"Did you have a date this weekend?"

I don't confide in Sheryl when it comes to my personal life, but that hasn't stopped her from poking around trying to uncover every small detail she can about it.

Since I don't see the harm in sharing, I answer truthfully. "I had a date on Saturday night."

"With him?" Her smile widens.

"Who?" I toss back with an even wider smile.

"Alexander Donato," she says his name slowly as if she needs to pronounce it clearly so I don't mistake it for another man's name.

Considering I haven't gone on a date in a couple of months, there's no confusion regarding the single and available men in my life.

Right now, Alexander is the only one on my radar.

I pick up a pen from my desk and twirl it in my fingers. "Yes."

"He likes you, Olivia." She pushes her glasses back up her nose. "I hope you like him too."

I do. I like him a lot.

CHAPTER TWENTY-THREE

ALEXANDER

IT'S BEEN three days since I've seen Olivia.

I don't buy into the idea that a man has to wait a prescribed amount of time to text or call a woman after a date.

I would have been fine calling Olivia as soon as I got home on Saturday night, but she needed space. The swift end to our date was proof of that.

She got in the taxi before I had to chance to kiss her goodnight.

I wasn't pissed.

I went home and jerked off in the shower. I fell asleep with a smile on my face. I woke up Sunday morning on a high.

That carried me through the day as I hung out with Phoebe and Alvin.

I've been working since then. Long rehearsals have eaten up the last two days, but it's been worth it.

The pride I take in guiding a talented group of musicians to the soaring heights of a piece of well-crafted music is unmatched.

I watch from my perch in the center of the stage as the orchestra thins. Each member has his or her own post-rehearsal routine.

Some of them dart out of the building; others take their time packing up their instrument.

Isla Foster falls somewhere in the middle.

She's a petite blonde with a level of talent I've rarely seen.

Her love of the violin is evident in each note she plays.

"Good job today, Alexander." She approaches me with her violin case in her hand. "You're one of the best I've ever worked with."

It's a compliment I don't take lightly. "Thank you, Isla."

Her face softens as she smiles. "If I had a vote, I'd want you to stay on in a permanent capacity."

I've heard the same from two of her colleagues.

New York has always been home to me. For years I wanted this job more than my next breath, but that's not the case anymore.

"Gabriel can't stop talking about opening night." She rolls her pretty blue eyes. "My husband may be your biggest fan."

"My sister would have something to say about that."

"We'd let them argue that on their own."

Before I can respond, her phone chimes. She glances down at the large black purse slung over her shoulder. "That's Gabriel. He texts me after every rehearsal to tell me what a great job I did."

I smile at that.

"I tell him that he has no idea whether I killed it or butchered it." She scoops her phone out of her purse. Her eyes scan the screen. "My husband is predictable, but not in the ways that really matter."

I read between the lines. They're an affectionate couple. Both times I've seen them together, his focus has been on her.

She types something into her phone before she gazes at my face again. "I won't keep you, Alexander, but I just wanted to say how much I love working with you."

"I'm enjoying it too, Isla." I give her a curt nod.

"There's one other thing." She studies her phone, not making eye contact with me.

"What's that?" I ask with a quirk of my brow.

"You have perfect pitch." She turns her phone's screen toward me before she starts playing an Instagram video of me in the Pink Parlor, singing to my heart's content.

"I try."

She laughs. "I need to get Gabriel down there. Every time he sings in the shower, I melt into a puddle. I'd love to watch him on a stage like that."

I huff out a laugh at the thought of Gabriel Foster at a karaoke bar letting loose.

"There's another video that the Pink Parlor posted the other day." Her fingers skim the screen of her phone again. "Gabriel said this woman works for him. Olivia Hull. She's gorgeous and she can sing almost as well as you."

I watch intently as the video captures less than ten seconds of Olivia's performance. Her body moves fluidly to the music. She's stunning.

My cock hardens from the reminder of what I felt that night when I was watching her.

"Were you there together?" Isla asks as the video ends.

"Yes."

She smiles brightly. "Next time you should do a duet. Something tells me it would be pure magic."

AN HOUR later I'm standing in the open doorway of Olivia's office with two cups of coffee in my hands.

I decided to make the trip to Foster Enterprises after I left the rehearsal hall. I made a quick call to Sheryl, Olivia's assistant, to find out how her boss takes her coffee.

One cream and one sugar.

I stopped at the café down the block from here, ordered the coffees and rode the elevator up hoping to hell that Olivia would still be behind her desk.

She's not.

She's standing, with her back to me, gazing out at the skyline of Lower Manhattan.

She's wearing a navy blue dress and her hair is pinned up in a messy bun.

Her phone is to her ear. As she talks about lace bras, her ass sways a tempting beat I can't ignore.

My cock can't ignore it either.

The jeans I'm wearing don't mask my erection. I don't want to hide it. I want this woman.

I clear my throat to get her attention.

The sound lures her head back with a turn of her neck.

"Oh, I…" she pauses to smile at me. "I need to go. I'll get in touch tomorrow morning to finish this up."

She nods before she lowers the phone and places it on her desk.

"Alexander." My name falls from her perfect pink lips. "Why are you here?"

I raise both coffees in the air. "It's time for a coffee break."

Her gaze darts to a clock on the wall. It's past four p.m.

and I have no fucking clue when she gets a break or if she even takes breaks.

"Have a seat." Her hand waves in the air toward two white leather chairs that face her desk.

I advance into the room, kicking her office door closed with a push of my shoe.

It slams shut.

"Come sit next to me." I point at the white chairs.

She looks at the office chair behind her desk. I imagine she spends most of her day in it, handling whatever issues come her way.

I can tell that she's good at what she does and that she takes pride in it.

She rounds the desk, lowering herself into one of the chairs. I take a seat next to her, handing her one of the cups. "One cream. One sugar."

Surprise flashes over her expression. "How did you know?"

"Intuition," I lie through a smile.

"Sheryl," she responds with a sigh. "Your attention to detail is impressive."

I lean close enough to her that I can whisper in her ear. "The better you get to know me, the more impressive it becomes."

Taking a sip from the cup, her eyes narrow. "What does that mean?"

"It means I'll take the time to understand every nuance of your body, Olivia. I'll make you come often. Intensely."

She coughs on a swallow, shoving the cup back at me. "You didn't just say that."

I place both cups on her desk. Reaching for her, I rub a hand over the center of her back as she coughs again. "I did and I meant every word."

She glances at my face, her breathing labored. "You're so sure that I'll sleep with you."

I slide my hand up her back, to her neck. I run my finger along the soft skin. "You will."

"You're cocky." She lifts a brow.

"Confident," I fire back with a lift of my own. "I'm confident that you want me just as badly as I want you."

Her lips part but she doesn't reply. Instead, she picks up her coffee cup and takes another drink.

She's flushed. Her nipples have furled into tight points beneath her dress. Her crossed legs are shifting restlessly.

"What are you doing tonight?" I rub my hands together. "We need to get to know each other better."

That draws the corners of her lips up. "I have plans."

"Don't tell me that they're with a man."

Her shoulders relax as she lowers the cup to her lap. "I'm meeting Kate for a drink."

"After that, you'll meet me for a drink," I tell her.

She tilts her head and pauses. "One drink."

"One drink," I repeat back. "You name the place and the time."

CHAPTER TWENTY-FOUR

OLIVIA

WHEN ALEXANDER WALKS IN, I'm watching from a table in the corner.

It's been hours since he left my office. I tried to refocus on work, but it was impossible.

Every time I'm in the same room with him, my resolve melts a little.

He may be arrogant, but he's charming.

From where I'm sitting it looks like he's charming a smile out of the red-haired woman who complained incessantly that her order wasn't made to her exact liking.

He holds the door open for her as she exits, calling after her that he hopes she has a great night.

I smile inwardly, waiting for the moment when his eyes lock on mine.

He rakes a hand through his hair as he scans the interior of this quaint tea shop.

The jeans he had on earlier are now paired with a black sweater instead of the blue dress shirt he wore to my office.

He looks casual and elegant.

When he finally spots me, I wave my hand in the air to signal him over. He points to the counter as if to ask if I want anything.

I hold up the cup of tea that I ordered when I arrived twenty minutes ago.

He nods, approaching the female barista. He says something to her that makes her face light up.

I glance down at the white plastic table I'm sitting beside. I don't blame her for grinning at him like that. He's a gorgeous man with a bare ring finger.

He exudes a level of raw masculinity that I've never experienced before. I instantly wonder if the barista senses it too.

"Olivia Hull, you're full of surprises."

I look up to find Alexander standing next to the table. "I thought we'd indulge in a good bottle of wine or beer. Earl Grey would be proud of us both."

His order is the same as mine. It's a medium cup of tea.

"I like to think outside the box." I motion for him to sit across from me. "Did you have any trouble finding this place?"

He looks around the eclectic shop. The walls are covered with orange paint and pink shelves which are home to a collection of antique teacups and saucers.

I consider it a Manhattan treasure. It's one of those hole-in-the-wall places that only local and loyal customers frequent.

"I've been here before."

The admission surprises me enough that it catches my breath. "You've been here?"

"Many times. I like the tea." He raises his cup in the air. "We have more in common than you think."

I laugh that away with a wave of my hand. "You're a conductor. I work in lingerie…"

"Stop right there." He leans back in his chair. "You work in lingerie as in you wear Liore lingerie to work?"

My pulse thrums. "You know that's not what I meant."

"But you do," he says boldly. "You're wearing Liore lingerie now."

I glance down at the red sweater and jeans I'm wearing. The large white scarf around my neck covers any hint of the skin on my chest.

"What color, Olivia?"

I sip my tea, ignoring the question.

He persists. "White lace? Black satin?"

"Pink."

He growls. A literal growl curls off his tongue. "Fuck."

"Lace," I say softly.

"Goddammit," he rasps. "Show me."

I laugh. "No."

"Show me," he repeats. "It can be the top of your bra. The strap. Hell, I'm game if you strip right here and let me see it all."

I glance over his shoulder at two women leaving. There are only a handful of people left. None of them are glancing in our direction.

"Give me something to remember tonight by." A sexy grin takes over his mouth.

I close my eyes briefly, wondering if I'm doing this because of the half glass of wine I had earlier with Kate.

When I open them, his expression has shifted to pure desire. Lust dances in his blue eyes.

I slowly unwrap the scarf from my neck, carefully tugging it free before I let it fall to my lap.

His eyes drop to the skin of my chest and the v that dives between my breasts.

I inch forward, slip my hand down the smooth skin of my neck, and then lower until it's resting between my breasts. I slide it under the left side of my sweater and pull the material back just a touch.

I look down at the faintest hint of pink lace.

"There's something we need to discuss, Olivia." His voice is low, thick and filled with the same need I feel within me.

"We will soon," I say as I drop my hand. "Soon, Alexander."

Sliding back on his chair, his jaw tenses. "It can't be soon enough."

———

"DO YOUR PANTIES MATCH YOUR BRA?" he asks as we stand on the sidewalk outside my building. We walked the three blocks from the tea shop. He insisted. I didn't argue.

I shake my head as I wrap the scarf tighter around my neck. "I'm not showing you my panties."

"Yet, Alexander," he finishes the sentence. "Yet."

"I wasn't going to say that," I point out with a finger push to the center of his chest.

In one swift movement, my hand is in his, resting against his chest. "You are thinking it."

I am. I think about it more and more.

I thought about it while we had our tea and he talked about an upcoming performance of the symphony. I listened to every word he spoke with rapt attention.

His voice is mesmerizing. As he was explaining about the

cadence of the music and the intensity of the string section, I drifted into thoughts of what he must sound like during sex.

The deep, ragged breaths he would take, the grunts, the growl that might escape when he comes. I focused on all of that while he smiled through a one-sided discussion about classical music.

"I'm thinking about the fact that I need to be in my office bright and early tomorrow so I should get to bed."

"I can take you," he offers with a lift of one brow.

A grin spreads over my lips. "That's not up for discussion tonight."

He steps closer to me. His hands leap to my scarf, untying it slowly until it's hanging loosely around my neck.

"Is a kiss?" His voice is a deep rasp.

My tongue darts out to slick my bottom lip in anticipation. "A kiss?"

"Let me show you," he whispers.

I close my eyes when I feel his lips crash into mine. His hand moves to the back of my neck, the other drops to my hip. He pulls me into him as he kisses me deeply, tenderly and in a way I've never been kissed before.

CHAPTER TWENTY-FIVE

ALEXANDER

SHE LETS me between her lips without any reservation. I take full advantage, gliding my tongue along hers, gently biting her lower lip.

She moans into our kiss, and I deepen it more. My hand slides down to her ass. I grab it, squeeze it and pull her closer so she can feel what she's doing to me.

Her breath catches when she grinds her body against my erection.

I could come. I swear to fuck I could come from the taste of her.

It's minty and fresh. She's pure heaven.

Her hands are on me now. One is wrapped around my neck, the other resting on my shoulder.

I want to pick her up, carry her inside, pin her against the wall of the elevator as we ride it up to her place and then I want to fuck her.

She pulls back a touch and I groan aloud. I don't care if she knows how she's making me feel.

"Alexander." Her eyes blink. "Not yet."

I nod through a rush of frustration. I've never had to wait this long to have a woman.

Hell, I rarely put in any effort when I meet a woman I want to take to bed.

A drink and a flirtatious grin are usually all I need to do to get laid.

"Olivia." I press my lips to the corner of her mouth. "You're killing me. My cock is as hard as steel."

She rubs against it. "I know."

I close my eyes. This woman knows how to tempt and tease me. I can't tell if she's playing with me or if her refusal to fuck me is based in a real need to have a connection before she shares her body.

"I'll go home and think about you." I pull her even closer, my lips whispering over the shell of her ear. "I'll stroke my cock until I come. That will all be for you."

Her eyes find mine. "You're going to masturbate and think about me?"

"I do it every day, Olivia."

"Every day?"

"Every fucking day." I nip at her bottom lip.

She winces. "You're not sleeping with anyone else?"

What the hell?

"Are you?" I push back, my hand dropping to her ass again.

She squirms under my touch. "No. I'm not."

Relief floods me, sending a new raging need straight to my cock. I'm so hard there's a persistent deep ache within.

"You're the only woman I want to fuck," I say so there's

no misunderstanding about how badly I need to be inside of her.

Her gaze falls to the front of my jeans. "I didn't realize."

"I won't push to come up to your place tonight." I draw her eyes back up with a hand to her chin. "But it's going to happen soon. You want it just as badly as I do."

This time she doesn't protest. Her chin moves under my touch. It's a faint nod.

I take her mouth again in a kiss. It's soft and lures a breathy sigh from her throat. "Goodnight, Olivia."

Her hand darts to her lips. They're pink and swollen. "Goodnight, Alexander. Sweet dreams."

I watch as she turns and walks into the lobby of her building.

"Sweet dreams indeed," I mutter under my breath before I take off down the street in search of a bar and a shot of something much stronger than tea.

———

"I THOUGHT you forgot about me, Alex." Alvin shoves a book into my hands. "I saw this at the library today. We can look at it together."

I catch Phoebe's eye from where she's standing next to her dining room table. Her bottom lip quivers. This is what she's longed for. She wants there to be a connection between Alvin and me just as badly as I want it.

I'd say that that book I'm holding is a strong start.

I glance over at Alvin as he takes a seat next to me on the couch. "Does this mean you're taking up the piano again?"

Looking back at his mom, he lowers his voice. "I want to learn how to play a song before mom's birthday."

I thumb through the tattered book of sheet music.

"Which song?"

He turns a page, and then another before he points at the book. "That one."

"Dinner's almost ready," Phoebe calls from across the room. "I hope you're both hungry."

I was going to skip the meal to go back to Manhattan. I planned to surprise Olivia at her place with some take-out. I haven't stopped thinking about her since we kissed last night.

When I dropped in here unannounced, Alvin was in his room working on his homework. Phoebe was grading papers, but she set that aside to talk to me about how much she misses Monte.

I wish to hell I could right her world.

She deserves everything she wants, including family dinners with her husband sitting next to her.

"Don't tell mom." Alvin slams the book shut.

I nod. "What I can do to help?"

He opens his mouth to reveal a toothy grin. "Teach me. I want you to be my new piano teacher."

I should tell him that I don't have time for that, but I'll make it work. If I have to give up a few hours of sleep and drag the orchestra down to the rehearsal hall at six a.m. I'll do it.

"When do we start?"

He's on his feet, bouncing in place. "You'll do it?"

"Anything for you, Alvin." I put a hand on his shoulder. "Whatever you need, I'm there for you."

He takes off toward the table. That kid just gave me a gift. He doesn't realize it, but I'll leave this house a happier man than when I walked in.

CHAPTER TWENTY-SIX

OLIVIA

I WATCH Kate as she takes a sip of the smoothie. Her eyelids flutter shut.

"It's good, right?" I tuck my yoga mat under my arm. "I told you it was worth the subway ride."

We came to Washington Square Park after our yoga class. We hadn't been in weeks, but when I woke up this morning with a sharp pain in my shoulder, I knew that I needed a good workout.

I could have experienced that last night if I had invited Alexander up to my apartment.

"It's amazing." She takes another drink. "We should find a yoga studio close to here so we can grab these smoothies as soon as we're done class. It would save us the subway ride and a lot of time."

Time.

It's the most valuable currency in Kate's life.

She busies herself at her bridal shop to avoid facing her

pain. Gage Burke, the man who broke her heart, damaged her in ways he may never be aware of.

She tells me often that she's put their breakup in her rearview mirror, but it's a lie.

Her days are packed with work, friends and whatever else she can cram into the remaining few hours before she falls asleep.

"There's one two blocks over." I point down the street. "I took a class there once. I liked it. I'll book us in for one next week?"

"That works for me," she chirps. "How did you find out about this smoothie cart?"

"The manager of the store on Fifth Avenue." I start to walk back toward the subway stop. "She stopped by my office one day to bring me one."

Kate falls in step beside me, bumping her yoga mat against mine. "She knows how to impress the boss. Did it work?"

I laugh through a nod of my head. "It worked."

She sighs softly. "You haven't said anything about what happened last night, Liv. You met up with Alexander after we left the bar, right?"

A chill races through me. I should have grabbed a coat before I left my apartment tonight. I'm relying on my off-the-shoulder sweater and my yoga pants to keep me warm. They're failing miserably.

"Where did you meet him?"

I smile, knowing that Kate will understand. "At the tea shop."

She laughs. "Our tea shop?"

I shrug. "It seemed like the perfect place. I wanted a cup of tea and it's close to home."

"It's also incredibly unromantic," she points out. "Was he disappointed?"

We stop to wait for the light to change before we cross the street. "He's a regular there."

"You're kidding?" She sways in place. "He's been there before?"

I return the smile of a man who stops next to us before I look back at Kate. "That's what he told me."

We cross the street in silence as soon as the light changes.

Once we're back on the sidewalk, she narrows her eyes. "Did anything worth mentioning happen last night or are you two still playing that game of cat and mouse?"

"We kissed."

She stops mid-step. "You kissed?"

I move out of the way of a woman pushing a twin stroller. I gaze down at the two little boys as they pass.

"How was it?" Kate nudges my side with her elbow. "Is he a good kisser?"

I don't hesitate because I know she'll pester me until I tell her. "The best."

Her lips curve into a smile. "You deserve the best, Liv."

I push her to start walking again. "I want to catch the next train."

"Did it go beyond a kiss?"

I shake my head. "Just a kiss."

She stares at me for a minute. "The best love stories always start with a kiss."

I glance around, looking at each person as they pass us by. "All love stories start with a kiss. Some end with a broken heart."

Her head tilts. "Don't be a pessimist. You kissed a hot guy. You're probably going to fuck that hot guy. If you focus too much on the future, you'll forget to have fun in the present."

"That's written on the side of your smoothie cup, isn't it?"

"Not the fucking part, but the rest..." she shrugs her shoulder. "The rest is."

I bow my head and laugh. "Thanks for the advice. I'll be sure to have fun."

"That's all I want." She starts in the direction of the subway. "I want that and all the details when kissing Alexander turns to more."

"That's not happening." I raise a finger in the air and wiggle it at her. "What happens in my bedroom stays in my bedroom."

She tosses me a look. "Make it happen soon, Olivia. At least one of us should be doing something in our bedroom besides sleeping."

———

ALEXANDER: *I want you to meet someone.*

I sit on the edge of my bed and read the text message he sent me again. He wants me to meet someone.

I reply in the most obvious way.

Olivia: *Who?*

I slide under the covers, pulling the thick blanket around me. I showered when I got home an hour ago. The chill I felt after yoga class was washed away under a hot stream of water.

I glance down when my phone chimes.

Alexander: *It's a surprise.*

Before I can type anything, he's sent another message.

Alexander: *Tomorrow at six.*

I didn't think I'd see him tomorrow, so I'm in.

Olivia: *Where?*

I watch the three dots bounce on the screen as he types a reply.

Alexander: *A car will be waiting for you in front of your building.*

Reading the message twice, I rest my head on my pillow.

Olivia: *Fancy or casual?*

His response is instant.

Alexander: *Casual. I'll see you tomorrow, Olivia. Goodnight.*

I drop my phone on my nightstand and close my eyes.

I have no idea who Alexander wants me to meet tomorrow, but I hope that the night will end with another kiss and maybe more.

CHAPTER TWENTY-SEVEN

ALEXANDER

"IS THAT HER? She's really pretty." Alvin peers out the window of the restaurant at the beautiful woman getting out of the back seat of a black SUV.

"That's her." Pride swells inside of me.

Olivia isn't my girlfriend. We've only kissed once. I consider us friends, but I don't know if she does.

None of that matters because tonight she's already garnered the approval of my nephew.

She glances at her reflection in the large wall of windows. She looks amazing in a pair of dark jeans, a pink blouse and a black blazer.

It's casual, but it's also sophisticated.

"Here she comes," Alvin announces as Olivia swings open the door and walks through.

She spots me immediately. The grin on her face is evidence of that.

When Alvin rises to his feet from the bench we've been sitting on, her gaze drops to him.

Her smile widens even more.

I stand and approach her with open arms. I pull her close for a quick embrace. "You look stunning, Olivia."

She steps back to look me over. Black slacks, white button-down shirt and a gray blazer. I'm still dressed in the clothes I put on this morning before rehearsal.

"I'm Alvin." Alvin needles his way in between us.

"I'm Olivia. It's nice to meet you."

Alvin crosses his arms over his chest. "You're Trey Hale's cousin."

Olivia's eyes slide to my face before she settles her attention squarely on my nephew. "I am."

"You're lucky," Alvin stretches the words across his tongue.

"I'm very lucky," Olivia agrees with a sharp nod of her head.

"Your table is ready, Mr. Donato." The hostess approaches us with three menus in her hands. "If you'll follow me."

Alvin takes the lead, Olivia follows and with my hand resting on the small of her back, I fall in step beside her.

———

"YOU PLAYED CATCH WITH TREY?" Alvin peers at Olivia across the table. "What's that like?"

"Scary." Olivia laughs. "It was a long time ago. He was just learning how to throw a ball."

"I'm learning." Alvin winds his right arm up as if he's readying to toss a baseball. "My dad and I play catch when he's around."

"Alvin's dad drives a truck," I say to clarify. "He's on the road a lot, but I heard that he's coming home the day after tomorrow."

"You heard right." Alvin takes a bite of his chicken burger. "I'll have three whole days with him. My mom said I get to choose what we do."

Olivia smiles softly. "Will playing catch be one of those things?"

Alvin chews, talking out of the side of his mouth. "Yep."

He's been open with her since we sat down. He ordered what she did, a chicken burger and a garden salad even though he always goes for a cheeseburger and fries when we come here.

He was quick to explain that his mom is handling parent teacher conferences tonight.

When Phoebe asked me if I'd watch over him, I happily agreed.

We spent the first two hours at the rehearsal hall. After introducing Alvin to a few members of the symphony, I sat him down at the piano so we could go over the song he wants to play for my sister.

He's got a lot of work to do, but he's committed to practicing before our next lesson.

"Do you think we could come here again, Alex?" Alvin rubs a finger over the corner of his lip to catch a drop of mayonnaise. "I'll bring my mom and you can bring Olivia."

I raise a brow to question Olivia silently.

She smiles wide and nods.

"It's a date." I hear the distant chime of my cell in my pocket. "I think that's your mom, Alvin. It's time to finish up and get home."

———

THIRTY MINUTES LATER, Alvin is holding tightly to Olivia's hand as we approach his house.

Once we exited the restaurant, I was prepared to grab a taxi. Alvin wanted to ride the subway.

Olivia was the deciding vote, so we took the train.

It was the right call. The string quartet on the platform was good enough to warrant a stop and listen from all three of us.

I handed the male violinist my card. He's young, but his talent is immense.

I'm hoping he'll follow up with me.

I can't offer him anything but free mentorship, but he has a gift. With nurturing it will turn into a career.

"There you are," Phoebe calls from the front step of her house. "Did you have fun?"

"Loads of it." Alvin drops Olivia's hand and rushes toward his mom. He stops short of the step even though her arms are outstretched.

"I missed you." She sighs, her hands curving to lure him closer.

"I missed you too," he whispers. "We'll hug when I go to bed, okay?"

"Deal," she says quietly. "Did you thank Alex and Olivia for taking care of you tonight?"

He nods several times. "I can take care of myself, mom. We were mostly just hanging out."

An eye roll is the response he gets from his mother before she turns her attention to Olivia and me. "Thank you both. I appreciate you hanging out with him."

"We had a lot of fun," Olivia replies with a glance back at me.

"I'm going to take him inside now." Phoebe's hand

reaches for the rusted handle of the storm door. "I hope you two enjoy the rest of your night."

"We will," I answer for us both. "I guarantee that we will."

CHAPTER TWENTY-EIGHT

OLIVIA

"LET'S SIT AND DISCUSS SOMETHING."

"Here?" Alexander's gaze volleys between my face and the playground we're standing next to. It's a block from Phoebe's house. We passed it on our way to drop off Alvin. "You want to have *the* discussion here?"

I nod slowly. "It's private, quiet. We can sit on the swings and talk."

"Or we can go to the bar two blocks over and have a drink and talk," he counters.

"Too noisy." I cover my ear with my hand. "I think this spot is perfect."

He surveys the playground. It consists of slides, ladders, a wooden platform, and a half-dozen swings. "If we're going to talk about going back to my place, I'll sit wherever the hell you want me to sit."

I take the lead, trudging through the sand in my heels until I plop my ass on one of the swing seats.

I look over to where Alexander's settled himself next to me. The moon's light is casting a shadow over his face. The only other light is near the entrance to the playground twenty feet away from us.

"You're ready?" he asks, his voice deep and tense.

I push back and lift my legs in the air, letting the cool air breeze over my neck. "I'm ready."

He sits in place; his legs crossed at the ankle as he watches me. "Are you ready to fuck me, Olivia?"

I swing higher, the air gliding over me. "Yes, but there are some rules."

"Rules?" He chuckles. "What's rule number one?"

I look down as I coast past him. "Condoms are a must."

"Always," he says without hesitation. "Rule number two?"

"You can't tie me up."

His eyes catch mine as I pick up my pace. "I won't need to."

"What does that mean?"

"You won't want to go anywhere once you're in my bed."

I shake my head. "Cocky."

"Confident." He pauses as he watches me float past him. "Rule number three?"

I slow because this is the most important rule to me. Condoms are vital, but guarding my heart is just as important to me as protecting every other part of my body.

"I just want to have fun." I push the toe of my shoe into the sand to slow myself.

Alexander reaches over to grab the chain of the swing, sending me twisting sideways before I stop abruptly. "You'll always have fun with me."

I tuck a strand of my hair behind my ear. "I'm not looking for anything serious."

His eyes catch mine. "We're on the same page, Olivia."

I let out a small breath in relief. "Do you have any rules?"

His hands jump to the collar of my jacket. He tugs me close before he presses his lips to mine.

The kiss is soft and sensual. His tongue glides over mine in a heated promise of what's to come.

"My only rule is that you tell me if it's ever too much." He rests his forehead against mine. "Promise me that."

I give him a quick kiss on the mouth. "I promise."

"Your place or mine?" He reaches for my hand.

"Your place," I answer quickly.

He tugs me to my feet. "We're not taking the train this time. It would take too damn long and I'm too damn hard."

I glance down at the front of his pants. It's clear that he's a large man in every sense. "What are we waiting for?"

He turns to face me, stalling in place. "I need you to know something."

My stomach knots instantly. Dread rushes through me. "What?"

"I would have waited even longer." He kisses my hand. "You're worth the wait."

"Thank you," I manage to say as my heart thumps inside my chest.

Wrapping his arm around my waist, he whispers in my ear, "Let's go."

I suck in a deep breath and take the first step toward a night I know I'll never forget.

———

HIS APARTMENT ISN'T a reflection of him. It's cold and sterile. The black leather furniture offsets the white tile floors.

There are walls of sheer curtains covering floor-to-ceiling windows that overlook the skyline of Manhattan.

Music is softly playing as we enter the space. It's something classical and grand, like the man who lives here.

"My fridge is bare," he confesses as he helps me slip out of my jacket. "I can call down to room service if you want a drink."

It's one of the benefits of living in an apartment inside of a hotel I suppose.

"I'm not in the mood for a drink." I place my purse down on a glass coffee table. "How long have you lived here?"

He slides his jacket off and hangs it next to mine on an ornamental coatrack. "Not long. I rented it once I knew I was coming back to guest conduct."

I nod, wanting to ask where his next adventure will take him. I know, from what I've read online, that he's a wandering soul. He's always on the move.

He may have roots in New York in the form of his sister and her family, but he's in demand on all corners of the globe.

I look over to where a piano is sitting in the corner, surrounded by windows. "Was that an addition that you requested?"

His gaze follows mine. "It came with the place. I had it tuned the day I moved in. I've played it infrequently since."

I want to hear him play but I want something else more.

I've never been brazen with men.

I'll admit to being vocal in bed. I steal my release before I devote myself to my partner's pleasure. Tonight is different. I feel uninhibited. I instinctively know that he'll accept me as I am. He'll fulfill any desire I have.

I sense he's a considerate, attentive lover.

"You want to fuck me, Olivia." He closes the distance

between us with heavy, measured steps. "You're thinking about it now."

"I came here for that." I remind him with a press of my lips to his. "It's what I want."

His hands are on my blouse before I can say anything. He takes his time on each pink pearled button, his fingers grazing every inch of my skin as its exposed.

"Pink lace." He growls as he uncovers my bra. "Pretty pink lace."

I moan when his fingers slide over my breasts and when he lowers his mouth to my nipple to bite it through the soft lace I hold back a scream.

"My bed," he whispers against the skin between my breasts. "Come to my bed."

CHAPTER TWENTY-NINE

ALEXANDER

WE DIDN'T MAKE it to my bed.

I couldn't get her clothes off of her fast enough.

I unclasped the bra to reveal two luscious tits with high peaked rosy nipples. Perfection.

Her jeans were next. I yanked them to the floor before I slid off her pink, lace panties and stroked her slick cleft.

She was wet, needy and the moan that whispered over her lips was too much.

I pushed her against the wall so I could drop to my knees to taste her cunt.

That's not what Olivia wanted.

She took a few steps to the left to the window, pushing herself against it until her tits and pussy were pressed against the glass.

No one can see her. I have no fucking idea if she realizes that or not.

"Taste me?" she tempts me with a wiggle of her ass.

I unbutton my shirt and slide it off in one quick movement. I fumble with my belt but give up when she parts her legs and I get my first glimpse of the glistening lips of her cunt.

I'm on my knees, my face pressed against her, my tongue gliding over the smooth skin.

The taste is addictive. The scent is intoxicating.

"There," she purrs when I flick her swollen clit with the tip of my tongue.

I'm like a starving man, going at her with fervor. I kiss, lick, suck, bite and take until she's writhing against the glass.

I pull back and stare at her. "You're so fucking beautiful."

"I need to come," she whines. "More, please."

Her ass tempts me again when she wiggles it. I part her cheeks, kissing each before I lick her again.

When I finally slide a finger into her tight-as-fuck channel that sets her off.

She chants my name as she comes.

I pepper her skin with kisses as her movements slow.

I take my time sliding up her body, stopping to press my lips to the center of her back before I drag myself to my feet.

Her cheek is resting on the glass, a mist forming next to her mouth. She's breathing heavy, whispering something I can't make out.

"Olivia." I push her hair aside to kiss her neck as my hand drops to her pussy. "Spread for me."

"No," she protests weakly. "Give me a minute."

"I'll give you one second," I hiss back. "One."

I push two fingers into her pussy, bowing her back as she screams my name.

"Fuck my hand." I kiss her neck again. "I want to feel you come on my hand."

Her hand drops to mine, holding it in place, and as I

watch her face, she comes again, this time almost falling to her knees.

————

I HOLD her in place until she stills. "Stay here. Don't move."

The only response she gives is a slight nod of her head.

I push my jeans and boxer briefs down on my way to the bedside table. I yank it open and tear at the box of condoms until I have one in my hand.

The package is on the floor in the blink of an eye, and my cock is sheathed.

My hunger for her takes over.

I press against her, my cock heavy and aching between the cheeks of her ass.

"I've been waiting for this." I run my fingers over her cunt.

She spreads her legs to let me in. I enter her slowly, giving her time to adjust to the length and the width of my cock.

Every inch brings out a new sound from her throat.

Once I'm balls deep, I slide in and out, circling her clit with my finger.

"Please," she begs. "Please, Alexander."

I move slowly. It's so achingly slow that I have to close my eyes and rest my chin on her shoulder.

I need this to last. I want to savor every second I'm inside this woman.

I'm so lost in my need for her that I swear to fuck I could come with one heavy thrust.

"Harder," she whispers against the glass of the window.

I reach up and pinch her nipple. "I want you to come on my cock."

She works herself over the length of my dick, using me as a tool to chase her release.

I bite back a groan when her hand falls to cover mine.

She's searching for her clit. She wants to help get herself off, but this is mine.

She's mine tonight.

I give in to my body's demand to fuck her.

I pound into her with furious thrusts, giving her what she needs and taking what I want.

Her hands claw at the glass when she comes; screams tumble out from between her lips.

It's all I need. I fuck her through my own climax, feeling her pulsing around me.

CHAPTER THIRTY

OLIVIA

"YOU'RE GOING to need to carry me back to my apartment."
I laugh as I fall onto his bed.

He flexes both biceps.

Wow.

Alexander has a gorgeous body. He's muscular, lean and
has more stamina than any man I've ever been with.

"I'm up for that, Olivia." He drops onto the bed next
to me.

His hand finds his cock. He strokes it once. "You sucked
me dry."

I did.

After we fucked by the window, I stumbled to the bed
while he used the washroom to dispose of the condom.

The instant he was back he was between my legs again,
coaxing another orgasm from me.

I returned the favor by sliding his cock between my lips.

"You should stay the night." He turns on his side to face me. "I want you to stay the night."

I graze my fingertips over his lips. "I need to go home."

"You want to go home," he corrects me with a wry glance. "Honesty, Olivia. That's all I ask for."

"I want to go home," I echo what he just said.

"Give me ten minutes to catch my breath and I'll take you."

I've never needed a man to escort me home after sex. I don't want that from him.

"I can get there on my own." I press a kiss to his lips. "Tonight was fun."

"Let's discuss when we'll have fun again." He circles the back of my neck with his hand, pulling me closer for a deeper kiss.

"When we'll have sex again?" I question in a whispered tone.

"When I'll fuck you again." His lips are on mine again.

I break the kiss and pull back. "If you kiss me like that, I'll want to have fun again now."

Before I can take another breath, his arms are around me, I'm flat on my back and he's hovering above me.

"One last time, Olivia." He kisses me slowly. "Let me hear you come one last time before you leave."

I run my fingernails down his back. "How can I possibly say no?"

———

A LOUD KNOCK at my door wakes me.

I reach to find my phone. I dropped it on my bed after I got home last night. I fell asleep before I could respond to

Kate's text message asking how my date with Alexander went.

"Olivia!" Kate calls from the other side of the door. "Are you in there?"

I haul myself out of bed and grab a pair of black sweatpants and a red T-shirt. I slip both on over my lingerie and head straight out of my bedroom.

I swing open my apartment door.

"That's a good look." Kate laughs. "Did I wake you up?"

"What time is it?" I try to rub the sleep from my eyes.

"Just past seven." Kate brushes past me.

She's already dressed and ready to face her day. The black pants she has on are topped with a white blouse. It's one of my shirts that I've been searching my closet for.

I make a mental note to apologize to the dry cleaner down the block. I accused them of losing it last week.

She heads straight for my kitchen. "I'm going to make coffee. You're going to tell me what happened last night."

"I had sex," I announce because that's the only information she's looking for.

It's the reason she's here at the crack of dawn.

My words turn her around. "I knew it."

It's obvious. I know my makeup from last night is still caked to my face. My hair must look like a bird made a nest in it.

I didn't bother to clean up once I was home.

I was exhausted in the best way possible. I lost count of how many times I had an orgasm last night.

"Before you ask, yes, it was the best sex I've ever had."

She busies herself with the coffeemaker. "Are you going to see him again?"

I inch closer to her, resting my hip against the edge of the countertop. "Yes."

The aroma of the coffee wafts through the air, brightening my mood instantly.

"Soon?" She laughs as she grabs two mugs from my cupboard.

"I hope so," I answer with a giggle. "It was fun. He's fun."

"You sound surprised, Liv."

Do I?

My initial assessment of Alexander may have been off base. He's cocky and arrogant, but he's also funny, charming and an incredible lover.

She fills both mugs with coffee before she heads to the fridge to get the cream.

I pour a splash in mine and then I scoop a spoonful of sugar into it from a bowl on the counter. "Thanks for the coffee."

She picks up her mug and takes a sip. "You're happy."

I nod. "I am."

"Good. Stay that way. You deserve it."

CHAPTER THIRTY-ONE

OLIVIA

DAMMIT.

I rub my hand over the tea stain on my red skirt. Sheryl assured me that it wasn't noticeable, but it looks like a beacon of my incompetence to me.

I've always told myself to bring an extra set of clothes to the office, but I never followed through.

I drum my fingers against my forehead to try and cement the idea into my memory, so I'm never caught in this situation again.

I'm on my way up to Cathleen's office.

Thanks to Kate, I got to work early today. No thanks to myself, the Earl Grey tea I picked up on my way to the office, spilled on my jacket and skirt on the subway. The only thing spared was my black blouse.

I cursed aloud which drew a few disappointed glances from the commuters sitting near me.

I silently apologized with a mouthed, "*I'm sorry,*" and a

shrug.

The stain on my skirt wouldn't have bothered me except now I'm going into a meeting that could decide my fate with Liore Lingerie.

I know Cathleen wants to discuss the position in London. Sheryl's secret informant in HR tipped her off.

The elevator doors open with a swoosh and I take a step off.

I'm always hit with a jolt of nervous energy when I take the trip up here. This is where the people who make the monumental decisions spend their time.

I know I'm good at my job and I help my division run smoothly, but it's not enough.

I want to take on a more challenging role in the organization and the job in London fits the bill.

"Olivia," Cathleen calls out to me. "You're right on time."

It's a habit I'll never break.

My mom taught me that the best way to show someone you respect his or her time is to show up when you promise.

I take pride in how punctual I am.

"Cathleen." I rest my hand on my stomach as I approach her.

I'm trying a diversion tactic. Maybe she'll notice the large gold ring on my finger instead of the stain on my skirt.

Costume jewelry is my favorite, especially when it serves a dual purpose.

In this case, it's an epic fail.

Her gaze hones in on the middle of my skirt, right where the stain is.

I resist the urge to explain it away. I'll take the *ignore and rise above approach*. If I dazzle her with my sparkling personality and vast knowledge about the company, maybe she'll forget that I'm clumsy.

She looks elegant in the black skirted suit she's wearing. The black dress shirt underneath complements the serious look she's going for.

Silver jewelry is the polishing touch.

"We're going to spend a few minutes with Gabriel." She rests a hand on my shoulder.

Shit.

I didn't realize I'd be coming face-to-face with the big boss today.

She leans in as we walk down the corridor side-by-side. "Don't worry about your skirt. Gabriel has strawberry jam on his lapel from breakfast. It's his daughter's favorite."

Turning to her, I breathe a heavy sigh of relief.

"It works to your advantage. We're not looking for perfection, Olivia. We're looking for commitment, and you're committed to rocking that look right now."

I laugh. "I'll run with that."

––––––

"TEA FOR YOU, OLIVIA?" Gabriel's assistant smirks as she hands me a cup of tea.

I run my hand over my skirt. "Thank you."

Gabriel reaches for his cup of coffee. "As I was saying, we're looking for someone who wants to grow with the company."

I've been listening intently to him since I sat down next to this conference table ten minutes ago.

Cathleen took a seat beside me. She's been quiet for the most part, blindly nodding her head in the appropriate places and smiling when she feels I need encouragement.

I haven't had to pitch myself yet, but I sense that it's coming.

"Tell me about your first day on the job, Olivia."

"My first day?" I question for clarification. "Do you mean my first day as the District Operations Manager or…"

His hand darts into the air to stop me. "Your first day as an employee of Liore lingerie."

"I was nineteen. I was hired to work as a sales associate at the boutique on Fifth Avenue."

A smile graces his handsome face. His dark eyes widen. "One of the stores you oversee now?"

I nod. "It was a wonderful introduction. I learned a lot there."

"You've worked your way up the ranks."

I've clawed my way up. I had to fight tooth and nail to land the position I have now. "I believe that hard work is the key to success."

"I believe that too." He gazes at Cathleen before he looks in my direction again. "Cathleen tells me that you're a dedicated employee. You envision a long-term future with us."

"I do," I agree with a smile. "I believe I have a lot to offer. I'm smart and I understand the market."

"I don't need to be convinced of that." He points at the open laptop in front of him. "You've improved employee turnover rates in the stores you're overseeing. Sales are up compared to our other boutiques in the region."

In the region?

I'm surprised. I've always kept my head to the grindstone, but I keep an eye on what's happening with our stores in the northeast. I had no idea that I was surpassing the expectations I set for myself.

"You can see yourself living in London?" He picks up the coffee cup and takes a drink.

I nod enthusiastically. "I can see that."

"It's a life-changing move," he points out as he lowers the

cup to the table. "Don't underestimate the changes you'd have to endure."

"I've given it a lot of thought," I assure him with a warm smile. "I would do wondrous things for the company in London. I'd make you proud, sir."

"I believe you," he says as he snaps his laptop shut. "You've given me a lot to think about, Olivia."

I take it as a sign that our meeting is over, so I push back from the table.

"There's one other thing." He moves to stand, straightening his black suit jacket.

I stand too. "What is it?"

"My wife and I are hosting a dinner tomorrow night to celebrate Alexander Donato's contributions to the Philharmonic."

I nod and smile as if I know exactly what he's talking about.

"I assume you'll be there?"

I don't know how to answer that. The guest of honor hasn't invited me.

Cathleen pipes up as she shoves to her feet. "I forgot to mention that Olivia is my plus one."

I shoot her a look of gratitude.

"Good." Gabriel picks up the laptop. "I'll see you both there."

As soon as he exits the room, I turn my full attention to Cathleen. "You didn't have to do that."

Her hands land on my shoulders. "I saw that deer in the headlights look on your face. I have no idea what's going on between you and the conductor, but we're going to that party and we're going to have a blast."

I don't argue. If she wants me there, I'll be there.

CHAPTER THIRTY-TWO

ALEXANDER

WHAT THE FUCK IS THIS?

I thought I was meeting Gabriel Foster for dinner at Axel NY. It's been a favorite restaurant of mine for years.

When he called me last week and suggested we meet up tonight, I was on board.

I don't have a lot of friends other than Jack. I'm not on the hunt for new ones, but Gabriel has become one by accident.

Our shared love of classical music is the foundation for a burgeoning friendship.

This isn't a dinner between two friends.

This is some fucked-up surprise party.

It's not my birthday. I didn't win any awards. I have no idea why so many familiar faces are staring at me as I walk through the entrance.

"You're here." Isla Foster rushes toward me dressed in a light blue sparkly dress that makes her eyes pop. "We wanted to do something special to show our appreciation for you."

A case of beer would have done just fine.

My gaze slides to where Phoebe is standing. She's wearing the same black sheath dress and pearls she always does when there's a special occasion.

I raise a brow to her for not telling me this was happening when I talked to her this morning. She tosses me a shrug and a smile.

I doubt like hell I look half as good as most of the people in attendance.

I'm wearing a navy blue suit and a pinstriped shirt.

I haven't shaved since I took Olivia to bed. Part of the reason was that I wanted her scent to linger on my face the next day. Today, it was pure laziness that kept my razor in the drawer in my bathroom during my shower.

I rake a hand through my hair. It needs a cut.

Gabriel approaches with a bottle of beer in his hand. "Your old friend, Jack, told me this was your favorite."

I look over his shoulder to catch Jack raising a bottle in the air. I'm tempted to flip him the bird, but there are too many people in this room who wouldn't find the humor in that.

Most of the musicians I work with are easy going, but a few take the job and themselves too seriously.

I scan the room examining every face. Some are familiar, others not, but one jumps out at me.

Christ.

I lucked out when I walked into this place.

Standing in the middle of the restaurant, dressed in a killer red dress is the woman I haven't stopped thinking about in days, weeks if I'm honest.

Olivia Hull is here.

Maybe this night will turn out better than I imagined it would.

———

"YOU LOOKED SURPRISED." Olivia takes the glass of champagne from my hand. "Did you not realize this was a party in your honor?"

I step closer to her. God, she smells incredible. It's a combination of the fragrance of her skin and a trace of perfume.

All that's missing is the scent of sex that permeated every pore of her body the other night when she was in my bed.

"I want to fuck you."

Her eyes widen. "Alexander."

"Olivia." I reach to touch her hand. "Now, who looks surprised? Did you not realize that I want to fuck you?"

"People will hear you," she lowers her voice.

I do the same, leaning in so my breath breezes over her cheek. "People have sex. Some people talk about having sex."

"Not here." Her head shakes.

I smile at the expression on her face. It's surprise mixed with desire. "There's a private room in the back. The door locks."

"How do you know that?" Her gaze narrows.

I tap a fingertip to my ear. "I've heard."

"Dinner will be served soon." She nervously taps her shoe on the floor. "I wasn't sure if I should come, but my boss invited me."

"Gabriel?"

"Cathleen." She gestures toward a woman dressed in a

knee-length navy blue dress. "She's a big fan of yours. She told me on the way over that she's been dying to meet you."

"I'm dying to eat you."

The corners of her lips twitch. "After the party. My place tonight."

"Something to look forward to." I place my hand on the small of her back. "Introduce me to Cathleen."

Her smile widens. "She'll like that."

"As your lover, Olivia."

"What?" Her eyes slide over my face.

"Introduce me to your boss as your lover."

A blush sweeps over her cheeks. "Are you?"

"We established that the other night when I fucked you raw." I run the tip of my nose over her cheek. "I'll remind you again tonight."

She turns to me, her lips hovering just over mine. "I welcome the reminder."

A tap on my shoulder lures my gaze back to catch Jack standing behind me. "Get to the front of the restaurant. Gabriel and Isla are waiting to toast you."

I nod abruptly before turning my attention back to Olivia.

She raises her glass in the air. "Here's to gentle reminders."

I move to rest my lips next to her ear. "Who said anything about it being gentle?"

She gasps; I kiss her softly and leave her with a promise of what's to come.

CHAPTER THIRTY-THREE

OLIVIA

IT'S BEEN MORE than an hour-and-a-half since I left Axel NY.

Alexander kissed me goodbye after he told me that he'd meet me at my apartment as soon as the last guest had cleared out of the restaurant.

I texted him thirty minutes ago to see if he'd be on his way soon, but I haven't gotten a response.

A faint knock at my door draws me to my feet. I've been camped out on my sofa watching Netflix since I got home.

I changed into my favorite black bra and panty set. I covered that with the black silk robe I treated myself with for my birthday.

I want to wow Alexander.

Tugging on the sash of the robe, it falls open to reveal my lingerie. I smooth a hand over my hair, run a finger over my bottom lip and swing the door open.

"Holy hotness, baby."

I roll my eyes at Kate. "It's you."

"I take it you were expecting someone else." Her brows perk. "Alexander Donato perhaps?"

I yank her hand to pull her into my apartment before I shut the door. "He's supposed to come over."

She watches as I tie the sash on my robe into a knot. "I'm not staying long. I stopped by to give you something."

"What?" I follow her movements as her hand dives into the large red leather tote that's slung over her shoulder.

She yanks out a book. "I got an advanced copy of the new Nicholas Wolf novel."

I crane my neck so I can get a better look at the cover. "You did not."

She holds the book up to give me the perfect view. "I did. Tilly got it for me."

I know that her friend, Tilly, is married to Sebastian Wolf, Nicholas's older brother. I didn't realize that Kate's friendship with her included a perk like this.

"He's my favorite." I reach my hands forward. "I'll give it back to you as soon as I'm done."

"You'll keep it." She flips open the cover. "There's a special treat in there for you, Liv."

My gaze drops to the book and the personalized inscription.

It's just my name, the word '*Enjoy,*' and the signature of one of the greatest detective novelists of our time.

Tears prick the corners of my eyes when Kate slides the book into my hands.

"Why did you do this for me?" I ask softly.

Her hand brushes against my forearm. "Friends treat friends. I know you'd do the same for me if you were friends with anyone who knows the Hemsworth brothers."

I laugh as I slide my hand over my cheek to brush away a tear. "I totally would."

"Especially anyone who knows Chris. He's my favorite."

I tap my forehead. "I'll store that to memory."

"I'll take off before Alexander gets here." She turns back toward the door.

I glance over at my phone on the coffee table. It's still silent. "Stick around for a bit. When he gets here you can make a quick exit."

Her bag drops to the floor. "I read the last page of the book on the subway on my way home from work. Do you want a spoiler?"

I lift a finger to her lips to silence her. "Don't do it."

She smiles. "I won't tell you how that story ends but the one playing out between you and Alexander tonight is going to have a very happy ending."

"If he ever shows up." I roll my eyes. "If he's not here by midnight, I turn into a grump and go to bed alone."

Her gaze drops to the watch on her wrist. "The man has exactly one hour to get his ass down here."

———

THREE HOURS LATER, I wake up with a start when my phone rings.

I fumble in the dark to find the lamp on the nightstand next to my bed. I turn it on, shielding my eyes from the bright glare of the light.

I pick up my phone and bring it to my ear.

"Hello," I whisper into it.

"Olivia?"

I rest my head back on the pillow. "Alexander? What time is it?"

"It's late," he pauses. "Very late."

"I was asleep," I state the obvious. "I'm going back to sleep."

There was a time in my life when I would have given up just about everything, including sleep, to accommodate a man.

I won't anymore.

I have an important meeting tomorrow. I need to be alert and rested.

"Wait." His voice is gruff. "I'm fucked up right now."

I move to sit up in bed. He doesn't sound like himself. His voice has a tremor to it that's not usually there.

"Is everything alright?"

He exhales audibly. "Alvin."

"What about Alvin?" I question before he can say another word.

I don't know his nephew well, but he's a good kid. He was sweet to me when we had dinner together. I've been looking forward to seeing him again.

"Phoebe got called away from the party right after you left. He was sick. She ended up in the ER with him. I went down there. It scared the fuck out of me."

"Are you there now?" I swing my legs over the side of my bed.

It's not like I'm going to rush down there, am I? I barely know Alvin. I'm not Alexander's girlfriend. I don't belong there.

"No, I'm here. I'm in the lobby of your building."

I pick up my robe from where I threw it on the foot of my bed. I slip into it. "I'll buzz you up."

CHAPTER THIRTY-FOUR

OLIVIA

I SHUT the door behind him once he's inside my apartment. "Is Alvin alright?"

He looks around my living room. "It's food poisoning. They're keeping him overnight for observation. Phoebe is staying with him."

I nod and gesture toward my couch. "Do you want to sit down?"

His eyes rake me from head-to-toe. "I'd like that."

I follow as he moves across the room. "Can I get you anything? I can make coffee."

He scratches his chin as he lowers himself onto my couch. "Sit with me."

Taking a seat next to him, I adjust my robe.

"Blue velvet?" he asks, running his hand over one of the cushions.

"I found it in a vintage shop," I say quietly. "It's the most comfortable piece of furniture I own."

He leans back and sighs. "I like your taste."

I look around the room. Nothing matches, yet it all fits together perfectly.

I've always decorated by my rulebook, pairing modern with vintage. My mom tells me that my style gives her a migraine whenever she comes to visit. I find it soothing and calming.

"Will Alvin be released tomorrow…I mean later today?"

"The attending physician told Phoebe that they'd kick him out at around noon if he keeps improving. I'll pick them up."

He's a good brother and uncle. "I'm glad he'll be alright."

"Me too." His voice quakes. "I've never seen him like that before. He could barely move. His eyes were sunken in. I wanted to help, but..."

I nod, not surprised that his voice trailed off. He looks exhausted. I offer the only other thing I can think of that will help. "It's late. You need to rest. You can stay if you want."

He raises his chin until our eyes meet. "You want me to stay?"

I want to comfort him. "Yes."

He pushes to his feet, yanking his phone from his jacket pocket. "I told Phoebe to call if she needs anything. I'll need to leave the ringer on high."

"You can put it on the nightstand next to your pillow."

A ghost of a grin floats over his lips. "Thank you for this, Olivia."

"Let's sleep." I stand and reach for his hand. "Come with me."

———

I'VE BEEN WATCHING him sleep for almost an hour. I woke shortly before six. I'm not used to sleeping next to someone else.

I found comfort in every movement he made. He tossed and turned until he finally settled on his back with his arm over his head.

He looks masculine and sexy with my blanket resting just below his stomach.

I can see the trail of dark hair that disappears out of view.

He's nude. He dropped all of his clothes on the floor before he climbed into my bed.

I tossed my robe onto a chair in the corner before I joined him.

He talked about Alvin and the teenage babysitter who cooked for him. She had gotten sick too, but she was released soon after she arrived at the ER. Alvin ate more of the fish she prepared for the two of them than she did.

When he laughed about Alvin never wanting to eat fish again, I joined in.

It was easy and fun and when he kissed me goodnight I felt the promise of more, but he put his head back on the pillow and drifted to sleep.

I reach to turn off the alarm on my phone. I know it's set to buzz in five minutes.

"You're not going to leave me here alone, are you?" Alexander's voice in the morning is pure sinfulness.

It's gravelly and thick.

I turn back toward it. "I was just about to wake you."

His eyes are barely open, his hair a mess. He's sporting a shadow over his jaw and a smile on his lips.

"Thank you, Olivia."

"For?" I ask so there's no confusion.

He motions me closer with his arm. I move quickly, resting my head against his chest.

I settle in, smelling the scent of his skin, feeling the roughness of his trimmed chest hair against my skin.

He circles his arm around me. "You let me stay with you."

I press a kiss to his chest. "You were exhausted."

"You were kind." He returns the favor by kissing my forehead. "I wouldn't have slept at home. I would have stayed up all night replaying the image of Alvin on that hospital stretcher in my mind over and over again."

"I'm glad I could help."

"Help me now." His voice drifts into a seductive tone.

I pull back and look up at his face. "How?"

His hand slides down his body, pushing the blanket away. His cock springs free, hard and curving up to his belly. He grabs the base. "Fuck me."

I stare at him; at all of him. I've never woken up next to anything like this before.

"I'll get a condom," I whisper as I slide off the bed.

He watches as I walk to my dresser. I tug open the top drawer and reach inside. I pull out a condom before I unhook my bra and slip off my panties.

"Hurry," he growls. "You can't walk around like that and not expect me to blow my load."

The room is darkened. The only light cast on me is from the hallway. "I'm coming."

"You will be."

I push the condom package toward him, but he shakes his head. "This time is for you. You sheath it. You ride it. You take what you need from me."

My hands shake as I rip open the package and fumble

with the condom. I suck in a deep breath before I roll it over his cock.

"Come here," he commands, tapping his chin. "I want you nice and wet."

I scramble up the bed and slide over him, straddling him. "Like this?"

"Like this," he echoes before he pulls me down onto his mouth.

CHAPTER THIRTY-FIVE

ALEXANDER

"YOU'RE A MILLION MILES AWAY." Phoebe's hand lands on my shoulder. "What are you thinking about?"

Who am I thinking about is the question.

The answer is Olivia Hull.

I spent last night at her apartment. I left her four hours ago and I haven't stopped thinking about her for a second.

She made me coffee after we fucked, joined me in the shower and when she got dressed for work, I sat on the corner of her bed and watched her every move.

I had no idea that watching a woman readying for her day could be so captivating.

Everything from the way she slipped into her white lace panties and bra to the way she brushed her hair made me want her even more.

I've never felt this way about a woman. The lust is consuming me, but there's a hint of something else there. I have no fucking clue what I'm feeling for her.

I step out of the way when a nurse rushes past me on her way down the corridor. I glance into Alvin's room again, but he's still in the washroom.

"Once Alvin is changed, we can go home." Phoebe drags a hand through her hair. "Thank you again for stopping by my house to pick up the change of clothes for us."

It was the least I could do.

That and the coffee I brought her along with a banana muffin. I knew she wouldn't put anything into her body since she refused to leave Alvin's side all night.

"How's Monte?" I ask because I know firsthand that he was a wreck last night.

I talked to him on the phone briefly before I left the hospital. He was near tears knowing his son was sick and he was over a thousand miles west of New York.

Phoebe's eyes close on a sigh. "I told him that Alvin would be just fine, but he's having a hard time forgiving himself for not being here."

I grab her shoulder and squeeze it. "He loves that kid more than anything."

Her eyes mist once she opens them. "I need him here, Alex. Dammit, I wish he could be here all the time."

I pull her into me for a hug. "You're both doing the best you can. Alvin's a lucky kid to have two parents who love him as much as you and Monte do."

She nods through a sniffle. "He has you too. You're staying in New York for a few more weeks, aren't you?"

I haven't laid out my long terms plan for her yet, because nothing is written in stone. I have a meeting this afternoon that will put more of the pieces of my future in place.

"I'm not going anywhere." I glance over her shoulder to the sight of Alvin waving both hands in our direction. He's standing next to the hospital bed where he spent the night. "It looks like your son is ready to hit the road."

She turns back, waving a hand in the air. "We'll be right there, sweetheart."

"Mom," Alvin groans. "I'm ten-years-old. I'm not your sweetheart."

I laugh. "He's feeling better."

"Let's get him home." She reaches up to adjust the lapels of my suit jacket. "It didn't slip past me that you're wearing the same clothes you were wearing last night."

I cock a brow. "You always did have an eagle eye."

She smiles and grabs my hand. "You smell like my favorite body wash. Monte got me a bottle from Matiz Cosmetics for my birthday."

"You wanted to be a police detective when you were a kid. You should have gone with that. Your investigation skills are impressive."

"I like Olivia." She squeezes my hand. "Alvin likes her. Be good to her, Alex."

"I'm starving," Alvin calls from behind us. "Can we please go home already?"

I look at Phoebe. "You heard the little man. It's time to get out of here."

She gives me a curt nod and a wide smile. "I couldn't agree with you more."

———

"FANCY MEETING YOU HERE."

I feel a tap on my shoulder with those words.

I'd know the seductive tone of that voice anywhere. I turn around eager to kiss her, but that's washed away when I realize she's not alone.

Olivia is standing on a sidewalk in Midtown Manhattan next to a guy in a three-piece suit. He can't keep his eyes off of her.

Who the fuck is this?

"Alexander Donato." I shove a hand at the dark-haired, blue-eyed schmuck.

He glances at Olivia before his hand lands in mine. "Derek Tocher."

I wait for someone to explain how the hell these two know each other.

"How's Alvin?" Olivia steps nearer to Tocher when a group of tourists pushes past her.

I take a step closer to her to even the distance. "Good. I dropped him and Phoebe off at home earlier."

Her eyes scan my face. "I'm glad he's doing better."

I glance over at Tocher who now has his eyes pinned to Olivia's ass. I clear my throat, but he doesn't even blink.

Asshole.

"Do you have time for a cup of coffee, Olivia?" I question as I step even closer to her. "Or tea?"

"We need to be somewhere." The bastard who is eye-fucking her responds.

"We have a meeting," Olivia chimes in.

"You're in the lingerie business?" I ask the dweeb, so he'll raise his head and look at me.

"No," he answers succinctly.

I shoot Olivia a look, but she's glancing at something over my shoulder. Times Square has a way of stealing the attention of everyone.

"It was good to see you, Olivia, and nice to meet you, Daryl."

"Derek," he corrects me with a smirk.

"I'll text you later." Olivia flashes me a cute smile.

I don't respond because *what the fuck was that*? I take off down the crowded sidewalk trying to brush off what just happened. My sole focus should be on the meeting I have in an hour because it's going to change my entire life, but all I can think of is Olivia and what the hell is going on between her and Derek Tocher.

CHAPTER THIRTY-SIX

OLIVIA

DEREK TOCHER HASN'T CHANGED at all since high school.

He's still the same annoying know-it-all he was back then. The only difference now is that he wears semi-expensive suits and too much cheap cologne.

I try to shift my stool to the left to gain more distance from him before I pass out from the fumes.

The other two women we're with don't seem to mind at all.

They've been laughing at his lame jokes and nodding in awe at every one of his stories about his success on Wall Street.

Unlike Derek, I do my homework.

I did it back in high school, and I do it now.

Derek Tocher is a junior broker with a small firm. He lives with his mom in Brooklyn and spends his extra time driving for Uber.

I should know. That's where I reconnected with him six months ago.

He told me about his perfect life as he drove me home from a fundraising gala. I looked him up online the next day. Those facts didn't lie, unlike Derek.

Derek recognized me as soon as I got in his mom's car. Admittedly it took me a bit to place him.

I wasn't popular in high school. He was. He was the all-star quarterback and the leading scorer with the cheerleaders.

I didn't make the cheer squad, so I was never on his radar.

"I wish my husband was more like you, Derek." Nancy, one of my former classmates swoons. "You're so funny and attentive."

I try not to roll my eyes.

"Should we get down to reunion business?" I flip open the cover of my tablet. "I made some notes since our last meeting."

Everyone at the table laughs.

It's the same reaction I get every time I come to one of these meetings.

Derek was the one who suggested we chair the committee for our tenth high school reunion. I was on board immediately because I'm all for meeting up with people I haven't seen in ten years to show them that I've finally got my life together.

Unfortunately, no one at these meetings is in any hurry to nail down the details because the actual reunion isn't for another year.

"You ladies will never believe who I met today." Derek takes a sip of his over-priced whiskey sour.

I stare at my half-full glass of free water.

"Who?" Tiffany inches forward on her barstool.

We're sitting in a barbeque restaurant in the middle of Times Square on a weekday afternoon. Tiffany's husband is the manager. That's the reason Derek is tossing back whiskey at warp speed. Everything is half-price for our party.

"Alexander Donato."

My head snaps up.

Tiffany clucks her tongue. "That hot-as-hell conductor of the Philharmonic? His billboard is right over there."

I glance out the plate glass windows in the direction she's pointing. Ironically, I got my first look at it an hour ago when I was talking to Alexander. I spotted it over his shoulder.

It was a surreal moment.

The photograph on the billboard does not do the man justice.

"We talked to him." Derek gestures in my direction.

"Do you know him, Olivia?" Tiffany asks excitedly.

"I do…" I hesitate, wondering if I should blow all of their minds by telling them that he's my lover.

I wouldn't be overstepping since it was Alexander who told me to introduce him that way to Cathleen last night.

Nancy leans her elbows on the bar. "I know someone who knows him."

I sense a story coming on, so I settle back on the barstool to listen.

"Do tell." Tiffany taps the bar. "Details, details."

"She's a friend of a friend. The night they met he took her home with him."

My stomach drops. I don't know what I was expecting, but this wasn't it.

"And?" Tiffany draws the word across her tongue. "Don't stop there."

Nancy looks around the almost deserted restaurant. "He fucked her all night. I'm talking every position, every inch of his apartment and from what she said, the man has a solid nine inches to work with."

I bow my head.

"It went on for a couple of months. One night she showed up at his place to surprise him. He answered the door in his underwear. A naked woman came out of his bedroom looking for him." She shakes a fist in the air. "He's a cold-hearted bastard."

"With a big dick," Tiffany whispers.

Derek clears his throat. "Not to brag, ladies, but for comparison purposes, I'm packing more than Donato."

Tiffany's hand lands on his knee. "You must have had a growth spurt."

"A growth spurt?" Derek questions her with a nervous chuckle.

"I was the head of the cheer team." Tiffany laughs. "We fucked the night of senior prom, Derek. I know what you're packing in your pants."

Derek is up and gone in a flash.

The two women next to me laugh as he bolts down Broadway. I stare out at the billboard of Alexander, wondering what I've gotten myself into.

CHAPTER THIRTY-SEVEN

ALEXANDER

DEREK TOCHER IS A SCHMUCK. He has nothing to offer Olivia.

"Who's that?" Jack peers over my shoulder at the screen of my phone and the headshot of Tocher from his brokerage firm's website.

"No one." I exit the site and drop my phone in my pocket.

"His mother would disagree with you." Jack pats me on the shoulder as he rounds his desk. "I've got everything together for you, Alex."

I watch as he drops a stack of papers on his desk. "Tell me this is the right thing to do, Jack."

"Do you want me to answer that as your friend or your financial advisor?"

"Both."

He falls into his chair. "It's the right thing to do. It's smart. You're not going to regret this."

I hope to hell I'm not.

I'm not a wealthy man. I'm not a poor man.

I'm comfortable with a little breathing room.

Jack's kept me on track because I pay him to do that. He's helped my money grow to the point where I can do something like this.

I can invest in my future, and other people's as well.

"You don't look convinced." He leans back in his chair.

I rest both hands on the edge of his desk, looking back at his open office door. His assistant, Everly, took off for the day when I arrived.

I have no fucking clue if she was off the clock or if Jack sent her on her way so we could discuss this in private.

Either way, I'm glad this is just between the two of us.

"I'm confident in what I'm doing," I say gruffly. "I put a lot of thought into it."

"I'm confident in it too." He picks up a pen and taps it against the edge of his steel desk. "You've come a long way, Alex. I have to admit, I didn't see this coming."

I didn't either, but I've learned recently that life doesn't give a shit about the plans you make. What matters is what you do with the opportunities you're presented.

"How soon can we get moving on this?" I point at the stack of papers. "Do I need to sign any of those?"

He hands me the pen. "Get comfortable. You're signing every last one of these."

———

I HAVE no idea what Olivia's definition of *later* is.

It's nearing eleven p.m. and I still haven't heard from her. Granted, I didn't reach out to her earlier. I spent the evening with Jack. After I signed documents until my wrist was numb, we went for a celebratory beer.

That turned into three beers and the brilliant idea to come to Olivia's apartment.

The doorman remembered me from last night. He also recognized me from the performance of the Philharmonic he attended last week.

One selfie later, and he let me come up to her place to surprise her.

I hope to hell I won't be the one in for a surprise. If I find Derek Tocher inside, I'll tear him apart with my bare hands. Or I'll fuck off and drown my sorrows in another few beers.

I knock softly on the door of her apartment.

Silence.

I knock again, louder this time.

Still nothing.

Hoping the third time is a charm I bang my fist against the door and call out to her, "Olivia, it's me."

The sound of a door opening behind me turns me around.

The sight of Olivia in a pair of black sweatpants and a blue T-shirt almost drops me to my knees.

Her hair is in a ponytail. Her skin is washed clean.

She looks fresh-faced and innocent.

She's breathtaking.

"What are you doing here?" Her brows pop up. "Did something happen to Alvin?"

I shake my head. I can't think. All I want to do is take her to bed. Hold her, kiss her, fuck her. I want to keep her.

Her gaze falls back to her friend, Kate. "I'm going to go."

Kate nods but doesn't say a word.

I stand to the side as Olivia unlocks the door of her apartment, turns on the light and beckons me inside.

"Why are you here, Alexander?"

I close the door behind me. "Who is he?"

"Who?"

"Daryl." I shove my hands into the front pockets of my jeans.

I had the sense to go home and shower before I went to Jack's office. I needed the time between my meeting and signing those documents to think about my future.

"Derek," she says the lowlife's name with a half-grin on her face.

"Did you fuck him?"

Her hands fall to her hips. "You did not just ask me that."

I repeat the question because I need an answer. "Did you sleep with him?"

"That's rich," she begins before she turns to walk to the living room. "That's so rich coming from you of all people."

What the actual fuck is going on?

I watch the defiant way her ponytail sways as she marches across the room. I want to twist it into my fist and yank on it as I fuck her from behind.

"Olivia, answer the question."

Her arms are crossed over her chest when she turns. "No."

I close the distance between us with steady, even steps. "Answer the question."

"Only if you answer a question for me first."

How the fuck did this turn into a negotiation?

I want to know if he touched her, so I agree with a brisk nod.

She steps closer to me, her eyes burning into mine. "How did you feel when your lover walked in on you and another woman? How do you think she felt to find you in your under-wear with a naked woman?"

I scrub my hand over the back of my neck. "What the hell are you talking about?"

Her finger jabs into the middle of my chest. "Let me

refresh your memory. You met a woman and you took her home that night."

I shrug. "That doesn't help."

She huffs. "You had sex. Apparently, you had a lot of sex for a couple of months and one day she showed up at your place and you were fucking someone else."

I stare into her stormy blue eyes. They're filled with passion and anger.

She's jealous.

She's scared too. It's there in her posture and the tremble of her bottom lip.

"You're talking about Lola." I exhale harshly. "It was her idea to keep things casual. She was fucking her boss. I was fucking... other women. She happened to show up one night when I had company."

Skepticism knits her brow. "You didn't cheat on her?"

"We were never exclusive," I say tightly. "She knew I was sleeping with other women."

She doesn't say a word.

"Her boss fired her that day," I go on, "he ended the personal relationship too. She took that frustration out on me when she came over and I wasn't available to..."

"To screw her," she finishes for me.

I nod. "I don't know who told you about her, but you only heard one side of the story."

She rubs her temples. "I didn't know."

I take a tentative step toward her. "If I were in a relationship with a woman, I would not fuck around."

She works on a swallow. "Are you fucking around now?"

"Are you?" I ask because I need to know if she's sleeping with Derek.

"No," she whispers. "It's only you."

I believe her. I see the truth in her eyes.

"Derek is a guy I know from high school." She rolls her eyes. "He was a dick back then. He's a bigger dick now."

Relief rushes through me. "That's good to know."

"We're both on the committee that's working on our tenth high school reunion, but the meetings are mostly Derek humble bragging about things that aren't true."

I huff out a laugh. "I could tell he was an asshole when I met him."

"You have no idea."

I study her face, realization hitting me. "You're planning your tenth high school reunion? How old are you, Olivia?"

"Twenty-seven."

"I'm thirty…"

"Five," she interrupts me again. "I read it on your website. You were born in New York City before you traveled the world. You won some very prestigious awards."

"When did you look at my website?" I cock a brow.

She turns to the side. "It doesn't matter."

"When?" I press.

Her bare foot starts tapping on the hardwood floor. "I don't remember exactly."

"Don't lie to me."

She stares at me, her mouth curving into a smile. "It was shortly after you left the boutique that first day."

That knowledge makes her want her even more. She felt the pull that day too. "I don't want you to fuck anyone else."

Her chin rises. "I won't if you won't."

I pull her close. Staring down into her eyes, I kiss her softly. "We have a deal."

CHAPTER THIRTY-EIGHT

OLIVIA

HE PRESSES his lips to my forehead. "I'm staying the night again."

I didn't think it was up for discussion. "I'm not going to argue with you."

He takes my hand and leads me down the hallway to my bedroom. I stop him when he reaches to turn on the overhead light. "That's too bright. I'll open the curtain and bring in some moonlight."

I cross the room and tug on the curtains, opening them wide enough that when we are in bed, we'll be able to see the skyline.

I turn back to find him sitting on the bed with my watch in his hands.

"Tell me about this." He lifts it in the air carefully. "You wear it almost all the time."

I take a seat next to him. "It's my most treasured possession."

"Did a man give you this?"

There's not an accusatory tone in his voice at all. It's curiosity. "It belonged to my dad. My mom had it engraved with their wedding date."

He turns it over to examine the back. His index finger skims over the brushed metal. "You never talk about your dad."

I could say the same to him, but I don't. Sometimes families are complicated. He has a close relationship with his sister and his nephew. They're the people who matter most to him.

"He died when I was young." I sigh. "I don't remember him, but that watch makes me feel close to him. I don't know if that makes sense or not."

His gaze catches mine. "It makes sense."

"The day I graduated from high school my mom gave me a box of things that belonged to him." I point toward the wooden box I keep on a shelf. "There's a silver pen, a couple of neckties, some cufflinks, and this watch."

"It suits you." He places it in my palm. "It's too big and masculine for you, but for some reason it suits you."

I run my finger over the face of the watch. "I've always felt that too."

"Do you have any siblings or is it just you?"

"Just me," I answer with a soft smile.

"You're an only child?" That draws his brows up.

I nod. "I like it that way."

He takes the watch from me and sets it on my nightstand. "Your dad would be proud of the woman you've become."

They're not empty words meant to offer me comfort. I sense that he means them. "I think so too."

He presses a soft kiss to my lips. "I'm going to make love to you, Olivia."

"Let me undress you." My hands move to the buttons on his black dress shirt.

His hands jump to cover mine. "Take off your clothes first."

I look down at my sweatpants and T-shirt. "A sexy strip-tease is off the table."

He laughs. "I'm only interested in what's underneath."

I slide to my feet and undress quickly. I don't stop until my black panties and bra are on the floor. I twirl once in place.

"Your body is beautiful." His hand finds my outer thigh. "I'm crazy about every inch of you."

I gaze down at him. "Can I take off your clothes now?"

He moves to stand too. "I'll help if you like."

I shake my head. "I want to do this."

I take my time, uncovering his body slowly, peppering his skin with kisses.

Once he's nude, I move to drop to my knees, but his hands grab my biceps, holding me in place. "Don't. I am so close to coming."

"I want to kiss your cock," I purr. "You want that, don't you?"

His hands slide to my waist. I'm on my back on the bed before I can form a thought. "I want to fuck you."

I watch him stalk across the room to my dresser. He yanks open the top drawer and digs out a condom. It's on his cock in an instant as the foil package flutters to the floor.

I moan when he crawls over me.

My legs move apart, he slides the tip of his cock over my cleft and in one achingly exquisite moment, he's inside of me, and everything else in the world falls away other than the need I feel for this man.

———

"TELL ME WHAT YOU WANT, OLIVIA." His breath floats over my neck. "I'll give you anything you want."

I open my eyes. I must have drifted to sleep after we made love.

Alexander was attentive and tender, whispering words to me about how much he loved my body, how good it felt to be inside of me.

After he washed me with a warm cloth and disposed of the condom, he crawled into the bed and held me in his arms.

"How long was I asleep?" I whisper.

"Not long." His fingers move to push a strand of hair from my cheek.

I do the same to him, trailing my fingers over his forehead. "Did you sleep?"

"No." He shakes his head. "I watched you."

I stare into his eyes, feeling as though my soul is bare. I'm starting to feel something for him. It goes beyond the desperate need for moments like this.

It's not just sex anymore.

Is this love?

He wraps his hand around the back of my neck. "What can I do to make you happy today, Olivia?"

I press my lips to his, lingering there as his tongue slips over mine. "This."

"I'd stay in this bed for eternity if it kept a smile on your face."

I grin from ear-to-ear.

"I know you have to go to work, but think about tonight." His fingers move down my back. "Think about what I can do for you after a long, hard day at work."

My back bows when his hand finds my ass. He squeezes it before his fingers move to my pussy.

I shift my leg, wanting to feel him inside of me.

"I can cook for you." His lips trail over my neck. "I can sing for you. I can dance for you."

"Play for me," I whisper through a moan. "I want to watch you play the cello."

One long finger slides inside my channel, another finds my clit and I close my eyes, savoring his touch and the sound of my name as he says it over and over again.

CHAPTER THIRTY-NINE

ALEXANDER

I HAVE PLAYED FOR ROYALTY, presidents, and celebrities. Tonight, I played my cello for the most important person in the world.

I played it for the woman I'm falling in love with.

Admitting that to myself hasn't been easy, but running from the truth is futile.

I've felt it for weeks. It was unfamiliar at first.

My experience in love is limited. I felt something for a woman once, but it can't compare to this.

I look over to where Olivia's sitting.

I brought a folding chair onto the stage of the rehearsal hall because I wanted her to feel the music.

If I had taken her home and played it there, the magic would have been lost in the cramped space and limited acoustics.

She hasn't said a word.

I finish packing my instrument back in its case, the entire time feeling Olivia's eyes on me.

Once I'm done I motion for a stagehand to take it. He'll carry it back to my office and lock it up.

It's a treasured piece to me. It was given to me by one of my early music teachers. At the time I wasn't tall enough to play it. I grew into it and its charm grew on me.

It's not perfect by any means, but it fits me like a glove.

"Alexander?"

I turn to find Olivia on her feet. Her purse is slung over her shoulder.

She's dressed, as any woman might be if they were coming to the symphony. She's wearing a simple black dress, silver hoop earrings and black heels. My hands braided her hair.

I did that after our shower this morning before I took her to work.

"Yes?" I ask as I approach her.

"Is it always that beautiful?" Her hand flutters over the center of her chest. "Am I supposed to feel it in here?"

I rest my hand over hers. "If I'm playing it correctly, yes."

"I had no idea." Tears well in her eyes. "You're so talented."

I swallow, my emotions warring with each other. I want to kiss her, hold her, take her to my office and fuck her. I want all of it.

"Thank you," I say simply.

She extends her hands, taking mine. "It's incredible how much emotion comes through the music. You do all of that with your hands."

I bring her hands to my lips, kissing each of her fingers. "Your hands convey your emotions too."

She tries to tug her hands free, but I hold fast to them, resting my lips against them.

"You speak with your hands." I smile wryly. "I don't think you're aware of it, but they move with your words. It's fascinating."

Her brow furrows, her nose scrunching up. "I don't do that."

I drop her hands. "You do."

"I don't." Her hand swings in the air.

I stop it in place with my fingers on her wrist. "Point proven. You're unaware of it. That's why I love it."

Her gaze falls to the floor. "Where to now?"

"You're hungry." It's not a question. I met her here at six. Unless she ate dinner at five, she's ready for a meal.

"Famished." Her hand rubs her belly.

It's another perfect example of her expressing herself without noticing it.

"I take it pizza is still off the table?"

Her arms cross over her chest. "I eat it if there's nothing else available."

"We're in New York City." I wrap my arm around her waist to lead her off the stage. "Everything is available here."

———

TWO HOURS LATER, we're both satiated. Good Italian food can do that to a person.

Olivia passed on the pizza in favor of linguine. I opted for the same. Watching the woman eat, and enjoy every bite was one of the most erotic experiences of my life.

"You'll come home with me tonight."

She's quiet for a minute as we walk hand-in-hand down a street in Tribeca. "I can't tonight, Alexander."

That stops me in my tracks. "Why?"

She looks down at her watch. "I have a phone meeting at four a.m. with an associate in London. All of my notes are at home."

"Four in the morning?" I start moving again, walking with slow even steps. I want to prolong my time with her.

Hell, I want her to invite me to sleep at her place. I'd make her coffee before the meeting, and breakfast after.

"I'll set my alarm for three and Uber back to your place with you," I offer.

"No," she replies with a curt shake of her head. "That's not necessary. I'll head home soon and we can catch up tomorrow."

I'm frustrated. My cock is irritated. I wanted to be inside of her tonight. "Why don't we stop for a nightcap?"

I'm grasping at any straw that will give me thirty more minutes with her.

"Another time?" She turns to face me. "This call is important. I want to get some sleep in so I'm rested and alert."

I cradle her face in my hands, brushing my lips over hers. "I hate the person in London who can't wait a few hours to talk to you."

She smiles wide. "You can't hate someone you don't know."

"I hate them," I repeat with a half grin.

She takes a breath and points up the street. "There's a taxi coming. I'm going to grab it."

"At least let me kiss you goodnight outside your building."

Her hand jumps into the air as she swerves around me to get the taxi driver's attention. "You're impossible to resist. I'll want you to come up to my apartment and I won't get a wink in before my call."

Fuck. I'm striking out at every turn.

I move to open the taxi's door as it comes to a stop next to the curb, but she beats me to it. She's settling onto the seat when I pop my head inside.

"Goodnight, Olivia."

Her hand cups my cheek. "Goodnight, Alexander. Thank you for the private show."

"Anytime," I whisper before I step back and shut the door.

CHAPTER FORTY

OLIVIA

THAT ABRUPT END to a date thing I keep pulling needs to stop.

I did it again last night when Alexander was trying his best to wrestle an invitation back to my place out of me.

I wanted nothing more, but I had booked the London call two weeks ago, and I didn't want to reschedule.

I also didn't want Alexander listening to it from my bed.

My apartment is small. It's too small to have a conversation in one corner without a person in the other corner hearing every word.

I'll make it up to him tonight.

"You're here bright and early." Cathleen taps her fist against my open office door. "How did the call go?"

I lean against my desk, holding a mug of hot coffee in my hands. "I think it went well."

I would be enthusiastic if I could remember more of it.

I tossed and turned until my alarm rang at two-thirty.

Once I was out of bed, I splashed cold water on my face, made a pot of coffee and waited for the phone to ring.

When it did, I slid into work mode and let myself be whisked into a ninety-minute conversation.

By the time it was over, I knew that I wouldn't be able to sleep, so I took a long, hot shower.

"We're narrowing the candidate list, and someone I respect made the cut." She circles a manicured nail in my direction.

Hope flickers inside of me. I've been looking online at London rental properties. I've brushed up on landmarks there and I've spent time going through my wardrobe to see what essentials I'd need to take with me.

"How's Alexander?"

Her question catches me off guard. The mug in my hand shakes. I turn to place it on the corner of my desk. "He's fine."

"Things are still going well between you two?" She taps her finger under her bottom lip. "I bought two tickets to his last performance. I'm taking someone special."

Since I didn't receive an invitation, I assume it's not me.

She fills in the blank with a smile. "It's Ted. He works in marketing."

I tilt my head, trying to remember what Ted from marketing looks like. "I hope you two will have fun."

"You'll be there, right?"

Twisting a strand of hair around my finger, I nod. "I wouldn't miss it for the world."

I might.

I don't have a ticket.

I imagine it's sold out by now, but more importantly, Alexander hasn't mentioned it.

––––––

"YOU'RE READING TOO much into it." Kate scoffs. "His last performance isn't for another two weeks. He'll invite you. I hope he invites both of us, but that's just this girl dreaming big."

I toss a piece of popcorn at her. She deftly catches it in her mouth.

"Am I reading too much into the fact that it's Friday night and we're sitting here watching Netflix?"

"You didn't finish that question," she pauses to wink at me. "You're wondering why your boyfriend didn't drop everything to spend tonight with you."

I tap one finger against her knee. "First things first, he's not my boyfriend."

"He is, but whatever." She rolls her eyes.

"Secondly, I don't expect him always to be free to see me."

"You do, but keep telling yourself that, Liv."

I drop my head back and laugh. "I do not."

"If you could have seen your face when he texted you to say he was busy tonight, you'd understand where I'm coming from." She tugs both corners of her lips down with her fingers. "Super sad face alert."

"I don't even know why I'm still awake." I look down at my watch. "I was up all night because of work."

"Work?" That lures her attention away from my television. "What kind of lingerie emergency happens in the middle of the night?"

"Asks the woman who slipped on a bra she left on the floor and cut open her top lip." I point at her mouth. "I vaguely remember sitting in the waiting room of the ER in the middle of the night while someone got stitched up."

"Point taken." She bows her head.

"I'm going to kick you out soon so I can sleep." I stretch my legs. "I might even pass out on this couch since I already have my pajamas on."

"Fine." She slides to her feet. "I'm taking the popcorn and my soda."

I curl under the blanket. "Lock the door on your way out."

"Dream about your boyfriend."

He might not be at the moment, but I want Alexander to be my boyfriend. I just don't know if he wants me to be his girlfriend.

CHAPTER FORTY-ONE

ALEXANDER

I MESS up Alvin's hair. "You're close, Alvin. You're so close."

He looks up at me with a beaming smile. "Do you think I'll be ready before mom's birthday?"

"You're ready now," I assure him. "Let's run through it one more time and then we'll take a lunch break."

He turns his attention back to the piano. His fingers drift over the keys, playing the song that is going to bring my sister to tears.

We've put in a lot of time and effort to get to this point.

I'd factor sacrifice in too.

Last night I gave up time with Olivia when Alvin requested an extra lesson. He sent me a text message after school asking if he could sleep over at my place.

It was a first. I rushed out to buy every sugary cereal I could find.

I stocked up on potato chips and candy and after we left

the rehearsal hall, he fell asleep in the Uber on the way to my apartment.

This morning he wanted fruit, so I ordered it from room service.

He stops mid-song to scratch his head. "Hey, Uncle."

I grab hold of the corner of the piano to steady myself. The rush of emotions that washes over me is almost too much.

"What's up?" I manage to get out without my voice cracking.

"Can Olivia meet us for lunch?" He trips his fingers over the keys. "Maybe at that place with the chicken burgers?"

That's music to my ears on this Saturday morning.

I type out a quick text to her.

Alexander: *Alvin misses you. He wants to know if you're available for lunch, say in thirty minutes?*

Her response is quick.

Olivia: *Is it just your favorite nephew and I or are you crashing this party?*

I laugh aloud, nodding at Alvin. "She's in."

"Yes," he says with a pump of his fist.

Alexander: *You want me there, Olivia.*

Olivia: *Cocky.*

I type one word and press send.

Alexander: *Confident.*

"Can we leave for lunch now?" Alvin swings his legs over the piano bench. "I'm hungry."

"Grab your coat." I point to where both our coats are slung over the back of a folding chair. "Grab mine too."

I type one last message to Olivia telling her where to meet us.

"Are you going to marry Olivia?" Alvin pushes my wool coat at me. "Mom says she's perfect for you."

His mom is right. Olivia is perfect for me.

Marriage isn't on my mind. Moving in with her is.

"Time will tell." Sliding on my coat, I pocket my phone. "Let's see if we can beat her to the restaurant."

He takes off at a run across the stage. "Hurry, Uncle Alex, I want to win."

I already won. My life can't get better than this.

———

"ARE you coming to my mom's birthday party?" Alvin asks after he finishes the last bite of food on his plate.

Olivia's gaze volleys between his face and mine. "Your mom's birthday party?"

Alvin gives her a brisk nod across the table. "It's the same night Uncle Alex gets fired."

Her hand leaps to her mouth to cover the broad grin.

"It's my last performance as guest conductor, Alvin," I clarify with a laugh. "No one fired me."

"I'm not sure," Olivia says tentatively, her gaze searching my face.

Dammit.

I haven't discussed my final performance with her. I assumed she'd be by my side that night as I close one chapter of my life and open another.

I reach to take her hand in mind. "There's a seat reserved just for you. I need you there, Olivia. I want you there."

A smile blooms on her full lips. "Of course, I'll be there, Alexander."

"Are you going to kiss now?" Alvin asks with a chuckle. "If you are, tell me so that I can cover my eyes."

I playfully swat him on the shoulder with my hand.

"We'll save the kissing for after we drop you off. Are you ready to go home?"

He moves the linen napkin from his lap onto the table. "I need to ask Olivia something first."

Olivia's brows perk as she turns in her chair, so she's facing him directly. "Ask away."

His hand scrubs over his forehead. "It's embarrassing."

"You can ask me anything. I promise I'll answer as truthfully as I can." Her tone is soft and comforting.

His eyes drop to his lap. "What kind of flowers do girls like?"

Olivia's gaze catches mine. She lifts a brow as her lips curve into a grin. "We like all flowers."

"There's a girl at school." Alvin scratches his chin. "Some kids in my homeroom aren't nice to her. They tease her."

"They're bullies," I pipe up.

He nods. "I don't like it. I want to help. Would flowers make her smile?"

He looks to Olivia to answer the question.

She does with grace. "They'd make her smile. They'd help her to see that she's not alone."

"She's not," he says defiantly. "I tell the teacher when I see her being picked on. Me and my friend, Chase, tell the kids who bug her to stop."

"You're a good friend to her." Olivia squeezes his shoulder.

"She's not my girlfriend." Both of Alvin's hands wave in the air. "I never said she was my girlfriend."

"Slow down." I chuckle. "Boys and girls can be friends, Alvin. No one said anything about her being your girlfriend."

"*She's his girlfriend*," Olivia mouths to me.

I nod before I look over at my nephew. "Do you know where she lives?"

"Two blocks from my house." Alvin holds up two fingers.

"Olivia will pick out some nice flowers at that shop your mom likes and we'll go deliver them to your friend." I reach for my wallet. "I'll pay the bill here and we can head there."

"We'll do it today?" Alvin shoots me a look of confusion.

"Today is the perfect day to put a smile on her face." Olivia pushes back from the table. "The flowers will put a smile in her heart too."

I stop and stare at her.

She wore a Yankee T-shirt and jeans because she knew it would put a smile on Alvin's face. She let him order her lunch and now she's giving him the courage to do the right thing.

If I had any doubt about what I feel for her, it's been erased inside this restaurant.

I'm in love with Olivia Hull. I'm the luckiest man on the planet.

CHAPTER FORTY-TWO

OLIVIA

ALEXANDER'S BREATH brushes over my inner thigh. I look down at his face. He's gorgeous. My bedroom is bathed in warm afternoon sunlight.

"I've never done this in the middle of the day," I confess.

"Good." He flicks the tip of his tongue over my clit. "We'll do it again tomorrow."

I tug on his dark hair, drawing his gaze up to me. "You make me feel so good."

He kisses my thigh. "I only want that. I want to make you feel incredible."

It felt that way when I came against his mouth. He's determined to make it happen again.

It will.

I'm already so close.

I wiggle my hips. "Lick me, please?"

"You're so polite." He blows a puff of air over my core. "Say what you mean, Olivia. Tell me to eat your cunt."

Both of my hands fall to my face, shielding my eyes. "I can't say that."

"Say it."

"I can't."

"You want it, don't you?" He buries his tongue inside of me, drawing a loud involuntary moan from somewhere deep within me.

I grab his hair and grind myself against his face.

He pulls back and I groan. "Don't stop."

"Tell me what you want." He rests his head on my thigh. "You've never been shy before."

That was because I wasn't falling in love with him. The sex was different in the beginning. My heart wasn't all wound up in it.

It's not just about chasing after an orgasm anymore. When I come with him, it touches the deepest parts of me.

I don't want to lose this or him.

"Come here." I beckon him closer with a curl of my fingers. "Kiss me, Alexander."

He slides up my body, his cock rubbing against my side.

He's so hard that I could mount him right now. I want that. I want to feel him bare inside of me.

I want things I've never wanted before.

His lips find mine in a slow, tender kiss. "Like this, Olivia?"

"Like this," I repeat back as I stare into his eyes. "There is something I want."

"I'll give it to you."

I swallow and gaze past his shoulder at the blue sky beyond my bedroom window. It feels right to talk about this now and not in the heated passion that consumes us at night when I can't see into his soul and mine is shielded behind my fears.

I'm not fearful anymore.

I can let myself feel.

I can allow myself to want something that my mom never had with the love of her life; a future.

I can risk a broken heart like the one she's carried inside of her all of her life. I will risk it to love this man even if it's only for a short time, although I want a lifetime with him.

"I've never made love without a condom." I don't break his gaze. "I'm on the pill. I have been for years. I'm clean. I had a checkup a few months ago and I haven't been with anyone since."

His eyes close on a heavy exhale and then he moves. I'm suddenly underneath him. His body is hovering over me.

My lips part and tears prick the corners of my eyes when he enters me without a barrier.

"Oh, God," I whimper when he starts to move.

"Fuck, Olivia," he whispers into my ear. "So fucking good."

He moves faster, increasing the pace, taking me to a place I've never been before.

I never want this to end.

I love him. I want him.

Alexander Donato is my future. He's my everything.

————

"DID you spend your entire weekend here?" Sheryl asks from where she's standing just inside my office. "You were here yesterday and now you're here bright and early on Monday morning. What's up?"

My future. That's what's up.

I was called in yesterday by Cathleen to discuss what comes next for me.

Sheryl must have heard about that from her friend in HR. That department is aware of every move I'm making. I'm not surprised that word is spreading around the building.

"I'm a dedicated employee?" I form it as a question. "It's that, or I can't get enough of the coffee in the break room."

She laughs.

I raise my mug toward her. "I can't take another sip of this. I'm going to run down to the café a block over. Do you want anything?"

"A minute of your time," she says quietly.

My head pops up. I search her face. "My time?"

"May I?" She motions to the chairs opposite my desk.

"Please." I nod.

She closes the door and takes a seat across from me. I'm tempted to point out that we've dressed alike again today. I picked a navy blue suit with a white blouse. She did the same. The only difference is the ruffle on her blouse.

"I know they've made a choice about London." She crosses her legs at the knee. "I also know the choice is under lock and key until the big announcement."

"The company is big on surprises. You know that, Sheryl."

"You can't give me a hint?" She perks a brow. "If you answer in a British accent, I won't tell anyone."

I laugh. "I'm not at liberty to give hints."

"Cathleen talked to you about it, right?" She pushes for more. "You know whether they picked you?"

I do know.

I was called into Gabriel's office this morning at the crack of dawn. Cathleen was there and the Executive Director of our London branch was on speakerphone as I heard the news.

"You'll know soon enough." I push up from my desk. "I'll go grab us those coffees."

"That's my job." She's on her feet too.

I shake off the idea with a brush of my hand. "I need the air. I'll be back in a few minutes."

She cups her hand over her ear. "Is that a British accent I hear?"

I shake my head as I grab my coat and my purse and head straight for the elevator.

CHAPTER FORTY-THREE

ALEXANDER

I SURVEY the interior of the old theatre I'm standing in. It's seen better days. It's been shuttered for more than a decade.

At one time it was a bustling off-Broadway venue. Amateur productions found their legs here. Some went on to win Tony Awards when they hit The Great White Way.

The building next door was abandoned as well. It used to house a music school.

It will again.

This time the name above the door will read The Anna Donato School of Music.

A name fitting a school that will nurture children's talent, just as my mother, Anna Donato, encouraged mine before she died of cancer.

She was a single mother, raising two children by working two jobs.

Her third job was teaching me how to use music to ease my pain after the death of my father.

This is her legacy.

My plan when I arrived back in New York weeks ago wasn't to put roots here, but things have changed.

It started when my former music teacher, Chris Morgenson, reached out to ask if I could help teach at the school he runs now.

I picked up a handful of classes for him when one of his regular teachers took ill.

That, and my time spent with Alvin, ignited something inside of me. I finally saw what drove my mother to insist I sit down behind the piano every night before bed to practice.

I want to teach.

The lease on the building where Chris is teaching now is due up in a month, so we sat down, worked out a deal and decided to launch under a new brand.

Chris will stay on and teach. He'll help me find my rhythm by walking me through the steps of running a school, and then he'll retire in a couple of years.

My goal is to teach next door. I'll offer classes to children of all ages. We'll work with families who can't afford to rent instruments or pay the lesson fees.

I'll supplement the work I do there, by the magic that will happen in this theatre.

My junior symphony will perform here, as will new talent from around the world.

People will pay to see what the next generation has to offer.

I'll guest conduct if the urge strikes and the finances need a boost.

I'll have plenty of help in the form of the teachers I've hired and my brother-in-law. I'm going to offer Monte a full-time job.

He'll be the man behind the scenes, taking care of everything from scheduling classes to fixing the broken railing on the stairs in the theatre.

It will keep him here, in New York, where he belongs.

The door at the end of the corridor opens allowing a sliver of daylight to slice through the darkness.

"Alexander?" Isla Foster calls out. "Am I at the right place?"

"I'm here." I turn and flick on the light switch, flooding the space with light.

She walks in with a smile. "I tried the door on the street, but it was locked up tight."

I didn't expect her this early. I know she has two daughters who need to be dropped off at pre-school. I suspected she'd show up closer to nine a.m., than eight.

"You're here early," I point out as she nears me.

"You're dirty." She laughs pointing at my dust-covered jeans and black T-shirt. "We have a lot of work to do to get this place into working order."

"You're in?"

I talked to her about this last week, asking her to keep it between the two of us. I need teachers and I went to her with that request in hand, asking if she knew anyone who would want to take a couple of afternoons out of their life to teach kids to play an instrument.

I plan to clean up the theatre in time for Phoebe's birthday so Alvin will be the second to take the stage when he plays for his mom in front of a crowd of his friends and family.

I'll be the first when I bring Olivia here later this week so I can play the piano for her and show her what my future looks like.

I'm staying in Manhattan to build a school, a junior symphony and a life with the woman I love.

"Of course I'm in." She brushes her hand over my shoulder. "I need to be in. Someone has to keep this place in order when you're jetting off to London."

What the fuck?

I laugh. "London? Why the hell would I go to London?"

Her blue eyes widen like saucers. "Oh shit."

"Oh shit?" I repeat back with a smirk. "Did you miss your morning cup of coffee, Isla? I'm as confused as you seem to be."

She shakes her head. "I'm not confused. You don't know, do you?"

My arms cross my chest. "I don't know what?"

"Olivia didn't tell you?"

My stomach recoils at the thought of Olivia keeping something from me; something to do with London, a city thousands of miles away from here. "Tell me, Isla."

"It's not my good news to share."

I stare at her.

"Fine," she says quietly. "She got the job, Alexander. Gabriel offered her the job in London this morning."

Joy covers her expression. She's obviously thrilled that Olivia took a job in London.

I can't process what I feel.

"He told me that she was the one last night." She looks to the left. "It looks like you're about to be a frequent flyer."

Like hell I am.

I can't breathe in this place. I need air and time. I need a fucking drink.

"I have to go." I push past her tossing her the keys. "Lock up when you're done."

"Alexander," she calls after me. "Try and act surprised when Olivia tells you."

I huff out a laugh as I swing open the door.

She didn't bother telling me she was chasing a job in London. If anyone is going to be surprised it'll be Olivia when I tell her that we're done.

CHAPTER FORTY-FOUR

OLIVIA

I STARE out my office window at Manhattan. I'll miss this view.

I can't see the Empire State Building or the Statue of Liberty from where I'm standing, but I can see apartments and office towers. When I look down, I spot hundreds of people rushing to get where they need to be.

I have a bird's eye view of the daily pulse of this city.

"Olivia."

His voice rushes over me, drawing goose bumps to my skin.

I adjust the collar of my blouse before I turn to face him.

"Alexander?"

I look at him. His hair is a mess. His T-shirt and jeans are covered in a layer of something that looks like cobwebs and dust. His skin is reddened from the cold. He must have been outside without a coat.

"Are you alright?" I ask as I approach him.

He enters my office and slams the door shut with his foot. "This is over."

His words send me back a step. "What?"

"I'm ending this today. Now." His voice is cold and even.

My bottom lip trembles. Ten minutes ago every single one of my dreams was coming true.

I was offered a new job this morning. My mom is coming to New York in two days to celebrate with me. I was going to introduce her to the man I love.

The same man who is now breaking my heart.

"Why?" I jut out my chin. "Tell me why."

"We want different things in life." He brushes his hand across his chest sending dust flying in the air. "I have a new focus."

A new focus?

That can only mean one thing.

"You're fucking someone else?" My voice breaks. "You're breaking up with me because you found someone new?"

My office door flies open.

His hand moves to shield his eyes as Sheryl barges in.

"Everyone can hear you two." She glances at Alexander before her gaze settles on my face and the tears streaming down my cheeks. "Rob called Mr. Foster. He's on his way down here, Olivia."

Fucking Rob. He's a junior assistant who is always in the middle of everyone else's business.

I don't care if he heard this. I don't care who hears this.

My life is changing forever. It's not supposed to be muted or tranquil.

"You can go, Sheryl." I motion toward the door.

"Gabriel just gave you a promotion," she points out. "Don't give him a reason to change his mind."

I curse under my breath for confiding in her after I got back with our coffees hours ago. I had to tell her. It impacts her life just as much as it does mine.

"I'm leaving. We wouldn't want your promotion to be in jeopardy," Alexander spits out. "I'm done here. We are done."

———

"WE WERE SUPPOSED to be celebrating your new job tonight," Kate says as she wraps her arm around my shoulder. "Not trying to mend your broken heart."

I sob against my hands. "Why does it hurt so much?"

"You love him," she points out in a whisper. "If you didn't, it wouldn't be this painful."

I've been stuck in the middle of my couch since I got home.

Mr. Foster gave me the afternoon off. By the time he got to my office, Alexander was gone. Gabriel caught me with tears running down my cheeks.

He didn't question the source, but told me that he wanted me to take the rest of the day for myself.

I did. I went to Kate's shop, cried on her shoulder, ate half a sandwich and then somehow ended up back here with her next to me.

"I'm an old pro at this." She moves to stand. "I helped Tilly when her heart was broken. I'm making us some tea."

I look down at the watch on my wrist. It's been a constant reminder of my mother's pain.

She never fell in love after my dad's death telling me that he was the love of her life, and that left no room for another man in her heart.

I feel that way now too.

Alexander owns every inch of my heart. I can't imagine it any other way.

"Is your mom still coming to visit?" Kate asks gently. "I can sleep on your couch. She can stay at my place if that works for the two of you."

It's a generous offer, but not necessary.

I know my mom will want to comfort me, but it will be in the form of retail therapy and midday movies.

She avoids her pain. She'll avoid mine too.

"I told her I needed to postpone the visit for a few weeks." I wipe away a tear running down my cheek. "I think I can handle things without her."

"You've always got me to turn to." She points to the kitchen. "I'll get the tea started. You stay put."

I'm not going anywhere.

The only place I want to be is with Alexander. He made it clear that we'll never be together again.

CHAPTER FORTY-FIVE

ALEXANDER

AS SHE WALKS into the theatre, Phoebe looks around. The last time I brought her here was the day I broke up with Olivia.

I needed my sister close to me. I didn't tell her why but she knew. She's always known when my world isn't right.

"You've been here day and night." She runs a finger along one of the handrails. "It looks like a different place."

That's thanks to all the volunteers who have come on board since I spread the word.

Musicians from the Philharmonic rolled up their shirtsleeves to pitch in. Local music teachers stepped up. Monte pitched in when he was home for a two-day stretch.

I offered him the job in front of Phoebe.

They cried. I cried. They had no fucking idea I was crying about Olivia and not tears of joy for the two of them.

Jesus, I miss her.

"I need to say something to you, Alex."

I lean against the handrail, closing my suit jacket with a button. "Fire away."

"Whatever happened between you and Olivia is killing you inside." She circles a finger in front of my face. "You think you're hiding it, but it's not working. Alvin asked me last night if you're sick."

Yesterday was Alvin's last rehearsal before tomorrow night. He'll be on this stage with a piano playing his heart out.

"I'm sick of the questions," I tease. "I cared about her, Phoebe. It takes time to get over that."

"What exactly broke you two up?" She eyes me suspiciously. "Was it you?"

I huff out a laugh. "Your faith in me is touching."

"I have faith that you want to find someone to share your heart with." She taps her fingers over my chest. "I have faith that Olivia is that woman."

I grab her hand in mine. "You're wrong. She's not."

Her eyes narrow. "Did she cheat on you, Alex?"

"No."

She thinks I cheated on her, or she did the day I showed up at her office. I didn't have the strength to correct her. She didn't expand on what Sheryl said about her promotion, so I stormed out.

She couldn't even bring herself to tell me that day that she was moving to London.

I expected Isla to say something. I know she heard that we broke up from her husband. Olivia's name hasn't left her lips since. The only topic of conversation she's interested in is what classes she'll teach and when she can start.

"I was hoping you would have made up so she'd be at my birthday party." She sighs. "I wanted to introduce her to Monte."

"That's not going to happen." I start down the staircase toward the stage. "She's in London."

———

THREE HOURS LATER, I'm standing in front of a flower stand holding back a rush of emotions.

"Is it okay, Uncle?" Alvin yanks on the sleeve of my jacket. "Can I get some flowers for Skylar too?"

Skylar. His princess. He's her knight in shining armor.

He protected her when kids bullied her and brought her flowers that Olivia helped him pick out.

That was weeks ago, but Skylar has become a constant in his life.

She's sat through three of his practices and was next to him when we went for chicken burgers and salad at the place where he confided in Olivia.

I ached for her that day.

I ache for her every damn day.

"Sure, bud." I wave my arm over the massive display of bouquets. "Choose whatever you want for Skylar, and something for your mom for her birthday too."

"Maybe if you pick something for Olivia, we can hang out with her again."

It's an innocent assumption, but flowers won't change a thing between Olivia and me.

"Olivia moved away," I remind him.

I've told him twice this week.

His bottom lip trembles as he looks up at me. "Does that mean if Skylar moves away, I can't be her friend anymore? I can't talk to her on the phone or go see her and bring her flowers?"

I look away, afraid of what my expression will give away.

"I'm sure if Skylar moved away, you'd still see her." I swallow. "What happened with Olivia is different."

"How?"

I can't explain it to him. I can't fucking explain it to myself, because Olivia is far different than any woman I've ever known, yet I've let the memory of someone else ruin my future with her.

I broke her heart before she had a chance to break mine.

I'm an asshole.

"What can I help you two handsome gentlemen with?" A woman who works at the flower market approaches us.

"We need flowers for my mom and for Skylar," Alvin answers with a grin. "I want something that will make their hearts smile."

The reminder of Olivia's words is too much. I turn my back to my nephew and close my eyes, wishing I could find a way to chase this constant pain away.

CHAPTER FORTY-SIX

OLIVIA

I GLANCE down at the silver frame in my hands. It holds the last picture that was taken of me with both of my parents. I'm too young to realize how lucky I was. I'm old enough now to understand it.

I place it on the corner of my desk.

I move it slightly to adjust it so when I'm in my chair, I can see it.

Standing back, I take in the space. It's freshly painted in a light gray tone. The marble floor gleams. The elegant chairs are the perfect complement to the white desk.

It suits me. It should. My name is on the door.

Olivia Hull. Regional Director of Operations.

"Boss?" Sheryl calls from outside my office. "You have your first official visitor."

I smooth my hands over the dark green dress I'm wearing. It's one of Kate's. She insisted I wear it on my first day.

"I'm nervous," I say quietly. "Who is it?"

She glances down at a pad of paper in her hand. "Phoebe Costa."

I look back over my shoulder at the late afternoon view from my large office window. I'm on the top floor of the building. All of Manhattan is spread before me including the iconic view of the Empire State Building. I've spent hours at that window while I was unpacking, wondering what Alexander was doing and who he was with.

I've tortured myself by imagining what his new lover looks like and whether he played the cello for her.

"She said it's personal," Sheryl clarifies. "Should I let her in or ask her to leave a message?"

"I'll see her." I move to stand next to my desk. "Can you bring her in now?"

She disappears out of view.

I suck in a deep breath. I wasn't expecting this.

It's been almost two weeks since Alexander ended our relationship. I stare at each face that passes me by when I'm walking down the street. I study the people on the subway, wondering if any of them know him.

"Olivia," Phoebe says my name excitedly as she steps into my office. "I hope it's okay that I showed up without an appointment. I asked about you at the reception desk in the lobby. I wanted to know how to reach you and they directed me up here."

"It's nice to see you." I beckon her in with my hand. "Do you want anything? Sheryl can get us some tea or coffee."

She glances back at Sheryl with a smile on her face. "I'm fine. Thank you for telling her I wanted to talk to her."

Sheryl backs away, waiting to close the door as Phoebe takes a seat in front of my desk.

I follow her lead and sit behind it.

"You're not in London."

I stare at her in silence. I hadn't thought about London since I turned Gabriel down when he offered me the position there. I told him I couldn't. I was honest in my reasoning.

I explained that as honored as I was that he saw me as the best candidate for the job, my life had changed since I applied for it.

I laid out a case about my value to the company and my contributions to its growth here in Manhattan.

I didn't mention Alexander, even though he factored into my decision. I had no idea where his future would take him, but I knew that mine couldn't take me away from him.

Gabriel understood and a moment after I turned him down for the job in London, he offered me the same job here.

It had just opened up a few days before. Fate stepped in and handed me everything I ever wanted. It only lasted for a few hours before Alexander left me.

"Alex told me you moved to London." She crosses her legs. "Why would he tell me that?"

I narrow my eyes. "I was offered a job there, but I didn't accept it. I couldn't accept it."

"Because of my brother?" Her eyes light up. "You love him, don't you?"

I see no reason to lie. "I do."

"He loves you too." She scrubs her hand over her forehead. "He's been walking around in a daze since you two broke up. It's none of my business, Olivia, but you belong together."

I don't know what he's told her about us, but I feel the need to clarify something, so she's not under the mistaken impression that his daze is caused by me. "He's interested in someone else, Phoebe."

"No way in hell." She shakes her head from side-to-side. "He's crazy about you."

I don't have a sibling, so I have no idea if they can sense things about each other. If they can, her sense is way off. "He told me that he had a new focus."

"The music school?"

I lean back in my chair. This is a hell of a first meeting at my new job. "What music school?"

Her eyes search mine for understanding. "Oh my God. I think I know what's going on here."

I wait for her to say something, anything that will help me understand.

"Alex must have assumed you were moving to London." She pushes to stand. "He was hurt by a woman who moved for a job. She chose it over him. It didn't end well."

I'm not responsible for his past choices. I'm also not that woman who hurt him. "He should have asked me about London."

"You should have told him you were up for a job there," she counters as any good sister would.

I smile. "I was undecided. I would never have said yes without speaking to him about it. Once I realized I was falling in love with him, I knew I couldn't make the move."

"Tell him this, Olivia." She gestures toward my office door. "I'll take you to him now, and you can explain all of this."

I wave her back down with my hand. "I can't, Phoebe."

"Why not?"

I glance down at the watch on my wrist. "We made assumptions about each other. We didn't trust what we were feeling. Maybe that's a sign..."

"No," she interrupts me. "It's bad communication. It happens to Monte and me all the time."

I listen in silence.

"Talk to my brother," she implores. "Tell him what you feel."

Exposing myself in that way isn't going to happen. I can't do it.

"I can't."

She nods. "I understand. I won't push, but please know that I've known Alex my entire life and I've never seen him this broken up before. He loves you, Olivia. He loves you with all of his heart."

I bite back an onslaught of emotion. "Maybe that's not enough."

CHAPTER FORTY-SEVEN

ALEXANDER

YOU'D THINK that my last performance as the guest conductor of the Philharmonic would be bittersweet.

It wasn't.

I was thrilled to exit the stage and change into a pair of jeans and a black sweater. I was in a rush to head here, to the theatre I purchased where the next chapters of my life will take place.

"Are you ready?" I bend down to look Alvin in the eye.

"I'm scared," he confesses. "What if I mess this up?"

"You wont," I reassure him with a pat on his back. "You've practiced for hours. You know each note by heart. You're going to own this, Alvin."

He nods. "I believe you."

"You need to remember who you are doing this for." I gesture at the large black curtain that separates the stage from the audience. "You're doing this for your mom."

"Is Skylar here yet?"

I smile as I move toward the curtain. "I'll check."

I peek out at the growing crowd. Many members of the orchestra promised they'd show. Some of Alvin's friends from school and their parents told me they'd be here for support.

I spot Phoebe front and center with Monte next to her.

His family is right behind them.

My eyes scan every row of seats looking for the familiar face of Skylar.

I see her. "She's here, Alvin."

Before I turn back, my eyes catch on another sight.

It can't be. I open the curtain wider and step out. Applause greets me. I shake it off with a wave of my hand.

"Alex," Phoebe calls to me as she darts to her feet. "Is it time?"

When I turn back to the beautiful woman in the red dress, she's gone.

Did I imagine that?

Did I just imagine Olivia standing in my theater?

I step back behind the curtain to find Alvin pacing back and forth. "I can't do it."

I get down on one knee and call him over. He towers over me. "You can. You need to remember that you're doing this for your mom, Alvin. This is her favorite song. It's her birthday. This is a gift she'll remember for the rest of her life."

His hand lands on my shoulder. "Are you ever scared, Uncle?"

I nod.

I'm scared I'll never see Olivia again. I'm scared that I've let my past steal my future.

"Do you promise it will be alright?" He scans my eyes for reassurance.

"I promise it will all be okay."

He bites his bottom lip. "Thank you for helping me with this. I love you."

Tears fall from my eyes as I pull him into me. "I love you too, Alvin. Go show them how it's done."

———

I'VE PLAYED "IMAGINE" thousands of times. I've listened to Alvin play it just as many, but I've never heard it the way I did tonight.

As my nephew took his time working through his mom's favorite song, I kept my eyes on him.

He was calm and confident.

He nailed each note and when he took a bow, every person in the theatre cheered.

"I'll be here for practice tomorrow, " Alvin promises. "When are we going to cut the cake?"

I had a chocolate cake delivered this afternoon from Phoebe's favorite bakery. "I'll run and get it. It's in my office."

I exit the stage and march past a dozen or so people looking over the posted schedules for upcoming classes.

Spots are filling fast.

We have all the teachers we need on staff, instruments have been donated and the building next door is almost fully painted.

I should be thrilled by the progress, but it's just another step toward a future without the woman I love.

"Alexander."

That voice. It almost brings me to my knees. I can't turn out of fear that I'm imagining it. It can't be her. She's in London.

"I'm sorry I didn't tell you about London."

I'm facing her before those words have left her lips.

Jesus, she's so fucking beautiful.

Red. It's her color.

"Olivia." I rush toward her. "I'm sorry."

She's in my arms, holding onto me, sobbing. "I went to Phoebe's house earlier. She told me to come here tonight."

We're in a corridor. No one is around but I need privacy. I need to be alone with her.

I hold her against me as we make our way to my office. Once we're inside I close the door. "You're here in New York."

"I've always been here." She looks up at me. "I never went to London."

"What?"

"I couldn't." She rubs at the streak of mascara under her eye. I push her hand away and slide my finger over it, brushing it away.

"Isla Foster told me Gabriel offered you the job."

"He did." She nods. "I turned him down."

What the fuck?

"You didn't go? You've been in New York all of this time?" I push back to look her over. "I felt you here. I swear to fuck I could feel you at times, but I told myself it was wishful thinking."

"You broke up with me because of someone else."

"No." I grab her forearms. "There was never anyone else. I wouldn't have fucked anyone else. I haven't since. I won't."

Her head shakes. "I'm not talking about that. Phoebe told me. She said you loved someone who left you for a job. That's why you ended things. You thought I was like her."

I'm an idiot. I let some forgettable woman from my past come between my future wife and I.

"I was scared," I admit. "I was so fucking scared that

you'd move to London, meet someone else, and forget about me."

"You're too cocky to think that way." She smiles. "Did you not realize that I was head over heels in love with you?"

"You are head over heels in love with me," I make the subtle correction.

"I am."

"I just launched this school and I'm putting together a junior symphony." I slide my hands to hers. "I knew I couldn't move to London with you right now so I saw it as the beginning of the end."

"You didn't have faith in my feelings for you." Her lips dip into a frown.

"You didn't tell me how you felt."

She works on a swallow. "You didn't tell me either."

"I love you," I say it clearly. "I love you more than I have ever loved anyone or anything in my life. I want you to marry me, grow old with me. I want it all."

"I feel the same way." Her lips brush mine. "But we have to be honest with each other to make this work."

"Agreed." I kiss her deeply.

"You should have told me about this place, Alexander."

"You should have told me about London, Olivia."

"No more secrets." She leans into me. "I got a promotion here in New York."

"I started a music school named after my mother." I brush a strand of hair from her face.

"We'll share everything." She takes my face in her hands. "All the good moments and the bad ones. We'll do it together."

"Hand-in-hand." I stare into her eyes. "Until death parts us."

CHAPTER FORTY-EIGHT

3 Months Later

OLIVIA

"HYPOTHETICALLY SPEAKING..." I stop because I know Kate is about to interrupt me.

She does, right on cue.

"Spit it out, Olivia." She rolls her eyes. "I have to get through my inventory check before we can go for pizza. I don't have time for your friend-of-a-friend stuff. What do you need?"

I glance out the window of her shop.

The sun is shining. It's the day after my birthday.

"A wedding dress," I answer softly.

She drops the veil in her hand and turns right around. "What?"

"Alexander proposed last night."

Her hand leaps to her mouth, her eyes instantly flood with tears.

I look down at my ring. It was Alexander's mother's ring. It's a beautiful pear-shaped diamond set in a platinum band.

"It's beautiful." Kate peers at the ring. "It's perfect."

She doesn't know how perfect. When he got down on one knee in our apartment, he told me I was his future. He whispered words about finding me in a sea of darkness. I'm his light, his hope and his promise.

When he slipped the ring on my finger, I fell into his arms.

We made love on our blue vintage velvet sofa and then in our bed.

I woke to a yellowed envelope on his pillow addressed to '*Alexander's Love*'.

The letter inside was handwritten by his mother days before she died.

I cried as I read each tender word about his soft heart and strong spirit.

I will cherish the letter until I take my last breath just as I'll cherish the man I'll marry later this year.

"You're getting married." She grabs hold of my shoulders. "You're going to be the most beautiful bride I've ever seen."

"You'll help me with everything, right?"

"Everything."

I suck in a deep breath. "You'll be my maid-of-honor?"

Her eyes search mine. "Really? You want that?"

"I need that." I kiss her cheek. "You're my best friend. I need you by my side when I say my vows."

"Inventory can wait." She claps her hands together. "Today we start trying on dresses."

———

"I MISSED YOU," Alexander says as soon as I walk into our apartment. "I made dinner for you."

He takes my sweater and hangs it up. I look over his shoulder. "You cooked?"

"You always say it as though you're surprised." He's on his knees, removing my knee-high leather boots. "I've cooked for you dozens of times since I moved in."

It's true.

I'm treated to his cooking at least a few times a week. On Sundays, we go to Phoebe and Monte's house. Sometimes they cook, other times Alexander takes to the kitchen, but it's always a delicious meal spent with our family.

His hand inches higher. It moves past the hem of my black skirt. "Tell me about your panties, Olivia."

He wasn't here to watch me dress this morning. He had an early meeting at the school with a potential investor.

He's expanding his classes to include adults. Those will take place during the day.

"They're pink." I look down and run a hand through his dark hair.

"Pink," he repeats back, gazing into my eyes.

His hand moves closer to my core. "Tell me more."

"I chose lace today."

He groans as his finger skims the inside of my thigh. "You know how much I love the feeling of lace on your skin."

I part my legs. "You know how much I love the feeling of your lips on my skin."

He leans down to press a kiss to my leg. "Here, Olivia?"

"Higher." I yank on his hair. "Much higher."

His hands move behind me, pulling the tight black skirt up. "Higher?"

I gasp at the rush of cool air as it hits my ass.

"I'm hard as nails right now." His tongue flicks the center of my panties. "I'm going to rip these right off of you."

"I like them," I whine.

"I love what's inside of them." With that, he pushes the triangle of lace aside and devours me.

EPILOGUE

6 Months Later

ALEXANDER

LIFE IS A SERIES OF CHOICES.

They lead us to our tomorrows.

I made what I thought was a foolish choice to spend a night with a woman I met in a bar.

That choice led me to a lingerie store and the woman of my dreams.

I'm staring at her now as she walks toward me with her mother by her side.

I've never seen anything more beautiful than my Olivia in her wedding dress.

It's simple, yet elegant, just as the love of my life is.

It fits her like a glove, even with the extra small bump in her middle.

No one knows yet that we're going to have a child in the

winter. A child we planned for and hoped for. We wanted to save that news for our reception when everyone, but Olivia, Alvin and Skylar, has a glass of champagne in their hands.

"Hi," she whispers as she nears me.

"*Hi*," I mouth back before turning to her mother.

I kiss her on the cheek because she raised the woman who changed my life. "Thank you for everything."

She smiles the same soft smile as her daughter before she moves to sit next to her sister in the front row.

We didn't opt for a church or a ballroom.

We are marrying in our theatre, on the stage where so many of our dreams have come true.

Jack is standing next to me. Kate is beside Olivia.

Alvin chose the flowers and the seat next to Trey Hale.

It's a celebration of our lives.

We turn to the justice of the peace, Chris Morgenson, my former music teacher and current business mentor.

"You've come a long way, Alex," he says to a round of laughter.

I nod. "I've come to where I belong."

Olivia sighs. "Where we belong."

"Shall we get started?" Chris opens the book in front of him.

The ceremony will be simple and straightforward. We'll exchange vows, I'll slip a simple platinum band on Olivia's hand next to my mother's engagement ring and she'll slide the platinum band we bought together onto my finger.

"Are you ready?" I whisper to her through the veil she's wearing.

"I've been ready since the day we met," she says quietly.

"Let's make this official," I say to Chris. "I can't wait to be this woman's husband."

———

OLIVIA

LIFE IS ALL ABOUT CHOICES.

When Alexander walked into the Liore boutique on Fifth Avenue that day, I chose to help him.

I didn't have to, but a part of me knew that it would change my life.

It took me on a path here, to the stage of our theatre and the dance floor that Alexander's students have created for us.

It's nothing more than a circle of flowers with the two of us in the middle.

The music playing is a recording of a piece by the junior symphony that my husband has been assembling.

It's off-key, hurried at times, but it couldn't be more perfect for our first dance as husband and wife.

As a family.

Our daughter will arrive in the winter.

Alexander doesn't know it's a girl yet. I told him we'd wait to open the gender reveal email from the doctor until tomorrow, but patience and curiosity don't mix well in my world.

I hope she'll have my husband's eyes, and his kindness.

I want her to possess his strength and courage.

I hope she inherits my compassion and openness.

"You're daydreaming about something." Alexander presses his lips to mine. "Tell me what it is."

"All of our tomorrows, " I answer simply.

It's the truth.

I know that life will change when our little girl arrives. We'll be settled into the two-bedroom apartment we bought a few months ago. I'll be working less. Alexander will be spending much of his time here, and I'll bundle our daughter up and bring her here so she can listen to her father play and teach.

"You love me more than anything," he says with conviction.

"I do," I say the words for the second time today.

He spins me around gently. I hear my mom hoot in the distance.

"You checked the email, didn't you?" He narrows his eyes. "We're having a daughter. I know it's a girl."

I stop to look up and into the face of the only man I've ever loved. "It's a girl."

Tears well in the corners of his brilliant blue eyes. "I don't know what I did to deserve this life."

I kiss his chin, drawing his face down to mine. "It's only going to get better from here."

He holds me close, so close that I can feel his heart beating against mine. "I know that it will because each day until my last, I'll wake up next to you, Olivia."

ALSO BY DEBORAH BLADON
& SUGGESTED READING ORDER

HUSH

BARE

WISH

SIN

LACE

THIRST

COMPASS

VERSUS

RUTHLESS

BLOOM

RUSH

CATCH

FROSTBITE

XOXO

HE LOVES ME NOT

BITTERSWEET

THANK YOU

Thank you for purchasing and downloading my book. I can't even begin to put to words what it means to me. If you enjoyed it, please remember to write a review for it. Let me know your thoughts! I want to keep my readers happy.

For more information on new series and standalones, please visit my website, www.deborahbladon.com. There are book trailers and other goodies to check out.

If you want to chat with me personally, please LIKE my page on Facebook. I love connecting with all of my readers because without you, none of this would be possible. www.facebook.com/authordeborahbladon

Thank you, for everything.

ABOUT THE AUTHOR

Deborah Bladon has never read a romance hero she didn't like. Her love for romance novels began when she was old enough to board the bus, library card in hand to check out the newest Harlequin paperbacks. She's a Canadian by heart, and by passport, but you can often spot her in New York City sipping a latte and looking for inspiration for her next story. Manhattan is definitely her second home.

She cherishes her family and believes that each day is a gift for writing, for reading, and for loving.